Books by Ben Masselink

THE DANGER ISLANDS
THE DEADLIEST WEAPON

THE DEADLIEST WEAPON

THE
DEADLIEST
WEAPON

By
Ben
Masselink

Little, Brown and Company
BOSTON   TORONTO

Published simultaneously in Canada
by Little, Brown & Company (Canada) Limited

PRINTED IN THE UNITED STATES OF AMERICA

For my Dad

The deadliest weapon in the world is a United States Marine and his rifle.

GENERAL JOHN J. PERSHING

Contents

THE DEADLIEST WEAPON

Operation FLINTLOCK

In June 1943 Paul was still safely in California, writing for and editing the *Pendleton Scout*, when the Joint Chiefs of Staffs directed Admiral Chester W. Nimitz, Commander in Chief Pacific Ocean Areas, to submit a plan for operations against the Marshall Islands.

The attack on the Marshalls would mark our first penetration of enemy territory. In the Solomons and the Gilberts we had but regained ground lost in 1942. At last the United States was making its first step forward into the islands which had been Japanese before 1941.

The Marshall Islands are coral atolls like the Gilberts, of which Tarawa was one. A coral atoll is a flat, sparkling necklace of low-lying islands covered with coconut palms, breadfruit and pandanus. These jewels surround a quiet lagoon, the atoll's own lake of sea.

To take such islands would compare with landing on a whale's back. There were no jungles or mountains where the Marines and soldiers could maneuver as on Guadalcanal or Bougainville. They must either exterminate the enemy within a few days or be thrown out.

The Marshalls then were the first big step on the road to Japan. The islands were "anchored aircraft carriers" whose planes could harass Allied shipping into the South Pacific. These carriers must be sunk to allow the war to be won.

In his bold plan for FLINTLOCK Admiral Nimitz decided to knife between the ribs of four strongly defended atolls with airfields — Wotje, Maloelap, Mili and Jaluit — and to pierce the very heart of the Marshalls: Kwajalein and Eniwetok.

The plan required three attack forces. The Northern to take Roi and Namur islands in Kwajalein Atoll, the Southern to take Kwajalein Island, and the Third Attack Force, which included the Twenty-second Marine Regiment Reinforced, to stand by as a reserve force during the assault on Kwajalein and then if not needed to pack up and go and take Eniwetok Atoll.

Altogether this Marshall Islands Joint Expeditionary Force numbered 297 ships, not counting the carrier task groups or the submarines. The assault troops numbered about 54,000. Of which Paul was one.

The Night Before

THEY WERE down below when the attack transport made the reef entrance at midnight and so they didn't know that they had passed from the open sea onto the dark glass of the lagoon. They heard only the shelling of the heavy cruisers and the destroyers and the pack howitzers, a faraway thunder. They were made to go below for security reasons, but for another reason too. The night before someone had presumably pushed Roark, the H. & S. Company's police sergeant, over the side. Anyway, he couldn't be found aboard ship and so this was the only conclusion. Roark wouldn't have jumped. A guy wouldn't do that. Or would he? With all his bluster Roark could have been frightened out of control. But it was more reasonable to believe that someone had given him a shove. Roark had no friends, only deep and muttering enemies, an occupational hazard of police sergeants.

Most Marines were on their racks. There was a poker game going on in the head. There was always a poker game going on in the head. For the most part the Twenty-second Marines were unblooded. No one but Kelton in this hold had been under fire before.

Those on their racks turned restlessly and sweated in the hot hold beneath the waterline of the steel ship. The racks were strips of canvas six feet long and two feet wide bound to lead pipe with tough, raw, yellow ropes. They were stacked one on top of each other in courses of five from deck to ceiling and were so close together that when a Marine lay on his back his nose brushed the lumped canvas above him. Because of the way the Marines were stacked this ship seemed to be transporting bodies. Leon had remarked on the twentieth night out, "When will they unshackle us, when do we bend to the oars?"

Paul slipped off his rack and down to the deck, almost putting his big foot in Leon's face. Up again for the sixth time this night, he was a tall, loosely jointed young man of twenty-three.

The head was brilliantly lighted. Water sloshed in the bowls. On the bulkhead were involved instructions on taking a shower and using as little fresh water as possible. In the middle of the deck five Marines played poker on a green blanket. Kelton leaned in one corner smoking, alone, watching, grin-

ning when he saw Paul come in. Paul looked at the
absorbed players. Dice or cards held no interest for
him but on a night like this he wished they did.
Gambling was something to tack your mind to. The
money could have been play money for all they
cared. The shoved twenty-dollar bills across the
green blanket with the casualness of maharajas.

Kelton moved over. "Restless, Sarge?" he asked
Paul. Kelton's usual expression was between a smirk
and a grin. He was too handsome. His lips were full
and curved and moist. Men mistrusted him; still they
had grave respect for his talent as a Marine and for
his rank of platoon sergeant. Although Kelton was a
Marine's Marine he was not a man's man. He was a
loner. He kept at it.

"You going to write a glowing 'I was there' story
tomorrow?"

Paul shrugged.

"What wave you going in?"

"I don't know," Paul said. "With H. & S."

"With H. & S.! You won't hit the beach until
after ten hundred."

Paul felt the heat rise in him. Why did Kelton
always make him angry? "That's where they put
me."

"It'll be over by then. You won't have anything
to write about."

"What do you mean, over? Look what happened

at Tarawa. It was two days before they could get off the beach. The fourteenth and fifteenth waves ran into as much fire as the first."

"Eniwetok ain't Tarawa. Eniwetok will be soft. It's being softened up now. Listen to the Navy guns."

Paul looked at Kelton. "So when you going in?"

"First wave. Easy Company."

"Yeah? I saw your name on the H. & S. roster."

Kelton grinned. "I didn't."

"What's the Lieutenant going to say about that?"

"I'll be back before they set up the CP. By that time I'll have had my fun. Want to come along?"

"You can't change an operational order to suit yourself." Paul couldn't help his voice's becoming desperate.

"What do you think the Colonel would say if he found out that instead of sitting on your can with all that dead wood of H. & S. you hit the beach with the first wave to secure his island for him?"

"I don't know about that. I just know each guy has a job and . . ."

"Job, ha! The typewriter, huh? The combat weapon." He moved over to the card game. "Deal me in."

Paul turned back for the hold. Kelton called after him. "See you on the beach tomorrow, Sergeant. I'll be waitin' on ya."

Paul walked back into the hold. Lighted by a ghoulish green bulb, it was twisted with tortured bodies in dyed green skivvies. The light seemed to be marsh gas wafting over them. Someone snored, someone coughed, someone groaned. Paul heard the distant thunder of the guns and strangely he thought of release, the feeling you get on a hot muggy summer night in the Midwest when it is difficult to breathe and you feel the sky is pressing down on you and then there is the flash on the horizon and the thunder has cracked open the sky to let the fresh air in and onto the spinning world. The thunder of the guns meant to Paul that soon they would escape from this smothering hold and would be able to breathe again. The hold was like the shell of an overdue egg. Paul longed to crack out before he turned rotten. Roark had cracked out, by himself or with help, the night before.

LeFort, dressed but for combat gear, slipped past him toward the ladder.

"Where you going?" Paul whispered.

LeFort didn't answer. He stumbled toward the ladder.

"You can't go topside," Paul said, catching his arm. LeFort tried pulling away and then Paul turned him around and he saw the gray, ruined face.

"Got to," LeFort said in a dead voice.

"Sit on the ladder a minute." Paul shook out a cigarette for him. LeFort ignored it.

LeFort said, "Rogers told me I got to go in with the Recon Company."

"How come?"

"I don't even know those guys. I was going in with H. & S., but Recon needs a sergeant and so Rogers says for me to go in with them." He rose suddenly. "I'm getting out."

Paul pulled him back.

"Roark didn't do it right. We're in the lagoon now. There are islands around I can swim to."

"With the enemy on them."

"Not all of them. You heard the dope. There are lots of islands in an atoll." Desperately LeFort grabbed Paul's arm. "I'm supposed to be their sergeant, those snooper guys. I don't even know those guys. I don't know how to snoop and poop. You know I been with H. & S. all the time I been overseas, Paul. I'm no line sergeant, not now. I'm recreational sergeant. I didn't go on any of those training hikes or maneuvers. I never even zeroed in my rifle. I'm not in condition. I haven't been schooled. I'm not like the rest of these kids. I'm a professional Marine. This is my life. Been in it twelve years. I like it."

"Take it easy, LeFort. Sit down, okay?"

LeFort's eyes were wild as he looked about the stinking hold. "We're prisoners! They got us locked in here. They herd us down like a bunch of cattle about to be slaughtered. And they don't give one damn!" He twisted away and ran up the ladder and crashed through the hatch topside.

Paul sat on the ladder. He looked at the Marines stacked in their racks, their 782 gear bound to the pipes, rifles slung, boondockers on the deck. They were all weapons of war. The rifle, the bayonet, the sheath knife, this ship, the boondockers, the meat can and cover, the big Marine Corps spoon, the poncho in the pack, the dyed skivvies, the dog tags, all of it, and most important, the men themselves. The men were the only unknown quantity of war. All other weapons, all equipment had been fire-tested. The helmet. The bayonet. The boondockers had been inspected by the Government and found to be sturdy and reliable. The rifle had been fired. But what of the men? What of him, Paul? What of LeFort? Yes, they had been examined by the Government and found to be physically and mentally sound. But was that enough? The M–1 rifle was sincere, honorable, gas-operated. This rifle was pure truth. But how would the men operate? How would this flesh and blood, this brain, these nerves hold up under fire? If you got sand in the bolt mechanism of the M–1 it wouldn't fire. With a toothbrush you brushed the sand out. But what if you got sand in your brain?

Yes, the men were the only equipment of war that had not been tried, tested, zeroed in and fired for record. Except for Kelton. He had been tested on Guadalcanal and he had passed.

LeFort came slowly back down the ladder. Paul said, "What happened?"

"Aw, it's a long ways down and I can't swim too hot and anyway there's a sentry up there who won't let you topside."

Paul moved back over to his sack, swung up into it and propped his head on his hands and his feet on the black portable typewriter case. He felt the thumping of the ship slow like a runner catching his breath and he knew that they were close, were deep in the lagoon closing in on the objective under the cover of darkness.

The thunder of the guns was louder now. Paul could distinguish between the Navy's fourteen-inchers and the Marine's pack howitzers. They had landed the pack howitzers the day before on a deserted islet and had immediately zeroed in on targets on Engebi.

Steadily the attack transport glided across the dark glass of the lagoon closer to the eruptions of flame from the Navy's big guns. They had all come through the gate of the atoll now — the transports, the destroyers, cruisers and battleships — and they stood waiting in giant force like too many policemen in the yard stepping on the flower beds.

Paul looked over and saw LeFort flat on his back staring at the bulging canvas an inch from his nose. Although Kelton's phrase "dead wood" was a rude one, it was perhaps true. Most all of them were dead wood in this hold and they were all needed to be just that. In an assault regiment such as the Twenty-second Marines there are three combat battalions plus a weapons battalion, and heading these the Headquarters and Service Company which includes the colonel and his staff, his exec, his operations officer, his intelligence officer, his quartermaster officer, the adjutant, the regimental doctor. Then the enlisted men topped by the regimental sergeant major. The cooks and bakers, the officers' bartenders, various orderlies, paymaster clerks, muster roll clerks, operations clerks, the intelligence section, company clerks, mail clerk, quartermaster clerks, police sergeant, recreational sergeant, PR sergeant and the pharmacist mates.

While the line companies were in training the people of H. & S. were busy behind their stoves and typewriters and it was not until the final maneuver before war that they participated. In an operation like this one, small-island fighting, it was not necessary to land stoves and typewriters. The assault troops must rout the enemy in a hurry or be pushed off the island. As a result H. & S. companies didn't have much to do but were lumped under what was called Command Post Security.

The Marine Corps assumes that every Marine is first of all a rifleman, a fighting man, because in boot

camp, no matter what his present job is, he has been
given a week of extended order drill and has been
trained, if fleetingly, in the use of the light machine
gun, has seen a gunnery sergeant take a BAR apart
and put it back together again, has thrown a dummy
grenade, has poked a dummy with a fixed bayonet
and has fired for record with an .03 or later with
the M–1.

Paul had never fired an M–1. He let his hand touch
his M–1 slung on the pipe of his sack. Rifle number . . . He had to lean over to check it to make
sure. 88625. He remembered his .03 as easily as he
remembered his serial number. 623856. And that
had been almost two years ago. There was a rifle.
That bolt-operated Springfield .03. He had enlisted
the summer before Pearl Harbor and the rifle issue
at that time was the .03. You knew where you stood
with it. He had fired sharpshooter on record day
and as soon as he had learned to love this simple and
accurate weapon it had been taken out of his hands
and a new, complicated, heavier M–1 put in its
place.

Paul heard Leon down below him scratching like
a mouse. Leon kept everything in ditty bags. He had
a ditty bag for his shaving gear, another for his toothbrush and paste, another for his wallet and letters,
another for his sewing kit. Everything was dropped
safely and warmly in its own little navy-blue ditty

bag. His mess gear sparkled, his dungarees were clean and pressed. He was the neatest Marine Paul had ever seen. He was a nesting Marine.

"Hey, Leon." Paul leaned over the side of his sack. "You hear about Kelton going in with Easy Company?"

Leon, a thin and polished-brown Mexican, smiled. "Great, huh? I was supposed to be scout for Easy Company. Now I stay in the rear echelon."

"I guess maybe Kelton's got the right idea. As much as I hate to admit it."

"He got rid of Roark anyway."

"Huh?"

"I bet. I bet he gave him the boot over the side."

"Aw . . ."

"That Roark was for nothing."

"Yeah but . . ."

Leon chuckled. "Or did you?"

"Me!"

"Sure. You hated his guts, didn't you? And he hated yours. Of course that could be said for all of us."

"Knock off the chatter, you guys," a Marine muttered.

Paul sighed and lay on his back, his feet propped up on the damn portable. Would a guy push another guy over the side two nights before an operation? Maybe this is just when he would do it. In peacetime this would be called murder. What would it be called now? What was another life when to-morrow . . . Paul found himself reading for the hundredth time what was written on the canvas above him in a childish scrawl.

> *Corp. Eddie Arno*
> *18th Engineers*
> *Youngstown, Ohio*
> *TARAWA 20 Nov. 1943*
> *Beginning: 204 men, 5 officers*
> *End: 24 men, 2 officers*

Three months before, Corporal Eddie Arno had stretched out on this rack where Paul was lying now, the battle over, and had printed that above him. Two hundred and four men reduced to twenty-four. That Tarawa must have been something. Paul was glad he had missed that one. Still what if you had been in it and out of it safely like Arno and had been able to write that. Out of just one outfit the casualties were almost ninety per cent. The Twenty-second Marines now but a couple of hours before landing had one casualty, Roark. Paul wished he could think deeper about Roark but he could not with an exploding world a couple of hours away.

He heard the swish of curtains. Kelton came out of the head and into the gloomy, stinking hold. He walked over to his sack and unslung his tommy gun

and worked the bolt. The noise crackled in the hold.
Kelton checked his gear. He wore a sheathed machete
on his combat pack instead of the bayonet. He had
cut his bayonet down and sharpened it and he wore
this on the webbing belt, heavy with the long clips
for the tommy gun. Kelton leaned casually against
the racks and went over his ammo, the grenades,
the rations in his pack, his life belt. It seemed to
Paul that this was all Kelton, a one-man, 165-pound
Marine Corps, carrying as much killing equipment
as possible and still able to move fast for that was
the Marine Corps way of fighting. Move fast. Mop
up later. The Marine Corps based their tactics on
a proven fact: The enemy was helpless without or-
ganization. So scatter them, break them up, let them
infiltrate as individuals and pick up these stragglers
later. The Army fought differently. They curled in
the holes and waited for air and artillery support
while the enemy reorganized. Kelton tested the
double edge of his bayonet with his thumb. He was
ready for any kind of fight, hand to hand, a fire fight,
demolition. He was a bomb.

But what if everyone took off like Kelton planned
to do tomorrow? Wasn't that being selfish? Everyone had his job to do, didn't he? And pure killing
was not the number one job for Kelton. Kelton
was staff NCO in charge of the regimental intelligence section. Under him he had six scouts, Leon

was one, who were attached to the line companies. It was Kelton's job, with his lieutenant, to coordinate these men and to see that they brought back word of enemy movements, prisoners if possible, and any captured charts or documents. It was a most important job. Because of Japanese charts captured on Kwajalein, this task force was able to pass into the Eniwetok lagoon.

Kelton was needed in the command post, but not until the Colonel got ashore and it was set up after ten hundred. Still, what if everyone took the war into his own hands like that, turned it into a personal war. Wouldn't things be in a pretty mess?

LeFort stared with his dead blue eyes at the canvas above his face. Leon fussed with his ditty bags. Why couldn't Kelton go in LeFort's place and leave LeFort in the rear echelon? That would make sense. You weren't supposed to smoke in the hold, only in the head, but Neff, the mail clerk, smoked, using three matches to light one cigarette, smoked and sweated, smoked and sweated. Someone snored, someone coughed, someone groaned. The shelling continued outside the bulkheads.

So at last they were going to war. Paul remembered playing war as a child in the long green backyards of Michigan. They would wear their dads' tin pan World War One helmets, too big, too heavy, rocky, smelly, and they used to play war under these helmets, shooting at each other with their fingers, "Bang, bang! I got you! You're dead!" Dead meant lying down on the cool grass and giggling. The awful smell of those helmets. The leather headband stained black from the long-ago war sweat. Paul touched his helmet now swinging above him with the new sweat on the band, his sweat, not his father's. Would some child ten years from now find this helmet in an Army-Navy store and make his dad buy it for him and play war with it? "Bang, bang, you're dead!" Would his child?

In his blouse, pants and leggings, the ugly snout-nosed tommy gun alongside him like a lover, Kelton, hair combed, not perspiring, with the small clever smile on his full lips, stretched out on his sack and waited. The poker game whispered in the head. Two hundred miles to the stern Roark's body lay suspended in the dark sea.

3

The First Day

T HE BOATSWAIN'S PIPE, a wet silver thread of ear-split, screeched through the hold. Then the raucous voice on the squawk box: "Reveille! Reveille! Out of those sacks, hit the deck! Reveille!"

Then the grumbling of the troops, even though most had not slept waiting for this moment which had come at last. "Only four hundred . . . Not morning yet . . . Still night."

Some stayed where they were and stared at the sack on top, others swung their bare feet down and into faces. Before it had been a hold of tightly stacked bodies, but now it was animated with bobbing heads and sick green skivvies and skinny elbows and pale white skin. You wouldn't think these were warriors.

Paul was trying to snake into his pants while still in the sack but the typewriter was in the way, it was always in the way. Below him Leon was already dressed in neatly pressed dungarees. When had he shaved? He smelled like civilian life.

Rogers, the First Sergeant, came down the ladder. "All right, line up for chow." The First Sergeant had never taken them to chow before.

Single file they mounted the ladder after the First Sergeant. It was different, in subtle ways, from a maneuver. The men were quieter, except for the few inevitable clowns who were always noisier in times of stress, like parrots. There was a politeness and respect about these Marines on this morning. No one jostled another. They were all made of glass and they knew it.

Paul was halfway up the ladder when he realized that he hadn't seen LeFort. He turned. LeFort still lay on his sack staring at the now empty canvas sling above him. "Hey, LeFort!" Paul yelled, but he was forced up by the men behind him.

The reason the First Sergeant came down to get them was to lead them through a maze of passageways deep in the ship to the mess hall. Always before they had found their own way by first going topside, then bunching up along the rail to move slowly down the starboard side of the ship and finally into the mess hall. This morning they didn't go topside where the guns were still firing, but padded along in the spooky passageways and stepped through hatches the size of oven doors and finally by this devious route, this mouse crawl, reached the steaming mess hall.

"Eat your fill, men." The First Sergeant grinned.

"Might be your last chance." Hostess-like, he stood just inside. "Seconds, thirds on everything."

Picking up the warm and moist stainless steel trays, they passed through the chow line. Looking down the line to the steam tables, Paul saw a difference. The messmen were freshly shaven, wore clean white T-shirts and white pants and were serving politely, not dumping and snarling. The mess sergeant clucked behind his men, nodding and smiling at the Marines in line, coaxing them, "Have another steak, son . . ."

It was unbelievable. They were serving steak and eggs. For breakfast.

"How many eggs you want, Sarge?" a messman asked Paul.

"Six," Paul said promptly and as a joke, never believing he would get them, but without hesitation the messman scooped up six eggs, three at a time, with his spatula and slid them carefully onto the largest compartment of Paul's tray so as not to break the yolks.

Hypnotized Paul gazed down at the eggs on his tray. Six bright orange eyes looked back at him. He hadn't eaten an egg, he hadn't even seen an egg or an eggshell in the seven months he had been overseas. He stumbled on through the line, his eyes held by the six brilliant juicy eyes, and then a crisp brown steak gently entered his field of vision to join the eyes. "Give him another," he heard the mess sergeant say, and another steak embraced the first. As the messman at the end of the line placed a mug of coffee on his tray, Paul looked up to see Leon slip one of his three steaks in a blue ditty bag.

They stood at narrow chest-high tables, stoking down the best food they had had in months. The thunder of the naval gunfire and artillery beat through the steel sides of the ship, while from above came a thin wire of noise, the dive bombers and fighters. The fabulous eggs, this golden breakfast, turned to cloth in Paul's mouth. He found the only way he could eat was to consciously move the muscles in his jaws. Pull up ligament M–1, number 2 to work muscle number 6385 to lift the jaw. Now carefully release all lines to lower jaw. Chew. Next to him the dainty Leon ate like a Chinese. Neff, the sweating mail clerk, pushed his tray aside and lit a cigarette with trembling fingers, using three matches. Paul could taste the sulphur in his own mouth. Kelton made a sandwich out of his extra steak and dropped it in the pocket of his blouse. The squawk box sounded off above their heads.

"All right, that first landing detail, report to your disembarkation station."

Kelton winked at Paul and pushed away from the table. "See you on the beach." Kelton left to go over the side and into an LCVP which would take him to an LST and then into the first-wave amphtracs.

Paul had thought that after chow they would be allowed topside. But the First Sergeant saw to it that they were all herded back into the hold the way they had come. LeFort had not moved. The First Sergeant yelled from the ladder: "LeFort! Didn't you get the word? Up to the net!"

"Yeah, yeah," LeFort said as if he were sleepy.

"Let's go then!"

Paul helped him get into his gear, the cartridge belt, the two canteens, first aid pack and combat knife. On his back he carried the light pack in which were poncho, two K rations, toilet gear, extra pair of socks. Strapped to it was the entrenching tool. LeFort looked sadly at the two bandoliers crisscrossing his chest. "All this ammo," he said. "Haven't fired that much in twelve years in the lousy Corps." He pronounced it corpse.

LeFort's face was small and gray and pinched under the helmet, an old man's face.

"They're making me carry an M–1," LeFort said, picking it up by its sling.

"Better than a carbine."

"Issue for staff and above is the carbine."

"LeFort ain't you up here yet!" Rogers yelled.

"See you on the beach," Paul said after him, watching him mount the ladder.

Paul always tried to pretend that his typewriter wasn't there, that he wasn't carrying it. At least the

Marine Corps could have covered that black case with some kind of camouflaged material that would make it look like war, the way they did the radios. The portable typewriter was exactly the way it had come from the factory to be bought by a father for his seventeen-year-old daughter so that she could type up her essays for English composition. However Paul had buckled a web strap onto the handle of the case so that he could loop it over his shoulder. He hoped it would work. He had never carried the typewriter down the net before.

The typewriter! He almost kicked it as he buckled the webbing onto the handle. How far from war could you get? The assault teams carried bazookas and mortars and flamethrowers and machine guns and satchel charges. He carried a typewriter.

When the men were all geared up they moved toward the forward part of the hold. In the head, the poker game continued. Leon, not sweating, neatly pressed, sat patiently as if waiting for the colonel's inspection at some Navy yard back in the States. Neff was in complete contrast, disheveled, unshaven, his dungarees black with sweat under the arms and on his back. He kept muttering about his mail. How could he ever catch up if they wouldn't allow him to sort letters. That's what he should be doing right now instead of this. This was foolish. Not his job. He should be on the command ship sorting letters with the brigade's mail clerk. That was his job. And the brigade's mail clerk needed him. He'd never catch up now. The men would give him hell for not receiving their mail. Well, it was their own fault.

The racks were all bare of gear and personnel. The Marines clustered at the forward part of the hold and ground their cigarettes on the deck. It would never have occurred to them to do this yesterday. In fact for the first time in their lives as Marines they did so, ground cigarettes out on a deck. Habit and discipline could never be as strong as this emotion they were all experiencing. They ground out cigarettes on a deck which just ten hours before they had kept as clean as a mess tray. Now they didn't care. Not even the toughest gunnery sergeant aboard would have reprimanded them. And too it was their unconscious way of getting back at the Navy, at the sailors who manned this ship. Those lucky guys would stay aboard, a mile from the singing shells and the mushrooming mortars and tonight they would eat hot chow and sleep on clean sacks. So here you go, buddy, this is what we think of you, the Marine's blood says as he grinds his cigarette out on the deck of a ship as if it were the face of the Admiral of the Fleet.

Through the steel sides of the ship they could hear the sputtering of the LCVP's and they knew the first wave had left this home to go to the LST's. "Boats away!" was the command given topside.

"Land the landing force!" A command unchanged since Caesar's time.

"What are they waitin' on?" a Marine complained. "Why don't they call us up?"

"Hurry up and wait."

"You going to write us all up, Paul? You going to make us all heroes?"

"Sure," Paul said. He was sitting on his typewriter. That was one thing it was good for.

"Get my name spelled right."

"I don't want to be a hero. I just want to be a live Marine. No. I mean I just want to be a civilian."

"Hell, mate, you're too fouled up to be a civilian any more."

The squawk box sounded. "Now hear this! Landing group Red report to your disembarkation station!"

"That's us."

The First Sergeant hollered down the ladder, "Let's go, you people! On the double!"

Someone ran into the head to get the card players. Up the ladder they all filed, their gear taut and silent. Dog tags taped, webbing tight, rifles easily on the sling, canteens bouncing with soft thuds. Each man was a weapon, a projection of his rifle. Up the ladder and finally for the first time in twenty-four hours they stepped out on open deck and into the fresh sea air.

The morning was gray and still cool from the

night. Before his eyes Paul saw the spectacle of war, a gray table of sea covered with the child's bathtub toys that make up a landing operation. Ships of all shapes and sizes. LST's, LCM's, LCVP's, AKA's. Destroyers, cruisers, transports. Sleek-looking ships and clumsy boats. All gray.

A landing operation, if everything goes right, is one of the most thrilling sights of a war. A landing operation is always the most difficult part of a war. One force, equipped with only what it can carry on its back, is going to attempt to come in from the sea where in its slow and awkward craft it presents a perfect target to the enemy. It is going to try to land and wrest this scrap of land from the hands of an enemy who has been fortifying it for twenty years. In the first place just to make the transition from sea to land is difficult. Hidden reefs, pounding surf, sharp coral, rip tides, strong currents, deep water. Men sink like stones with forty pounds on their backs. Now added to all this are artillery fire, mortars, light and heavy machine guns, 20mm guns, rifle fire, grenades.

The gray ships on the gray sea. The smoking island of Engebi. Or could it still be called an island? A haze of explosion hung over it, enveloping it, grayish yellow, heavy, gritty.

"Move along," the First Sergeant said to Paul. Paul lingered, held by this island of Engebi, the enemy, the target, the objective.

This regiment had been held in floating reserve in the Kwajalein operation a week before so this was not their first sight of an enemy atoll. But Kwajalein had not looked so destroyed as this. As they steamed up the lagoon of that largest atoll in the world they had seen the lovely surrounding islets, waving their slender, girlish coconut palms. But poor Engebi's palms were shattered. One or two tousled heads hung from broken necks. The rest were like splintered telephone poles.

One heavy cruiser lay regally off the island's eastern point and now decided to speak the way she had spoken to the island during the night. First a hot orange billowing cloud of flame came from her guns, the concussion wrinkling the sea in red waves before her, the sticks of her guns recoiling smoothly before the orange flame turned to white, then gray, then black smoke. Count to twenty-eight. One, two, three, four . . . twenty-eight. And Paul heard her voice and on the island he saw the innocent spurts of her shells.

Between him and the island Paul saw the amph-tracs, reptile-low in the water, fumbling about, getting into position at the line of departure. Kelton crouched in one of these with the assault troops, as did LeFort. What of LeFort? What were his thoughts now?

SBD's and F4Y's were over the island like flies over the dead, peeling off to strafe the beaches, the tracers winking out of their wings. SBD's dropped bombs as slow and large as seabags which later made dull thuds in Paul's ears. And there was the marvelous whoosh of rockets. Magically they appeared out of the wings, then seemed to snap back into them briefly as if they were on rubber bands before they shot ahead fast and faster to hit the beaches in a shower of Fourth of July sparks.

Two destroyers, like worrying dogs, kept moving off the west point of the island, skimming about smoothly, bow waves white, firing and firing again, moving so close in it seemed as if they were trying to grab the island by its tail the way they would a cornered coon and, shaking their bows, drag it into the lagoon and sink it. Yes, why didn't the island sink? After this bombardment Paul expected it to let up one final sigh of steam, a little cry, and disappear before his eyes. But it remained. He could see the trembling of its coral flesh after every attack. If it didn't sink after such an assault how could anything still remain alive on or under its skin?

Dumbly Paul moved up with his company toward the bow of the attack transport. All these magnificent ships were held in the glassy pocket of an enemy lagoon. What if the atoll tightened like a noose to squeeze, then crack the ships like eggs in a vise?

"The bow net," Neff muttered. "Why do we always draw the bow net?"

"Because we're not combat troops, mate," Leon said. "They got to give us a little danger too."

At the railing Paul looked down at the circling LCVP's bobbing in the chop, coxswains at the sterns, gunners by their weapons. The bow was not only the highest point of the ship, but it was also concave, so that the net, instead of hugging the sides of the ship, dropped straight through the air for over forty feet.

"First wave must have landed," a Marine said.

Paul saw the cruiser turning slowly away from the island, unable to fire any more with troops ashore, her part of this war over, a great lady leaving the party before it got maudlin and rough. The destroyers too, as if catching another scent, raced off to the left and away. A few curious planes remained above the island. They seemed intrigued and fascinated by the view below, like people stopping and pulling over on the shoulder of the highway to gape at the scene of an accident. The first wave was ashore. Marines were on enemy soil trying to get a foothold. Paul wished he could see. It was all a yellow haze.

"All right, you people, let's get into some kind of order here!" the booming voice of their captain rolled toward them.

The Captain was a big, white-haired man. On his head the helmet fit like a skullcap. He strode up to his company, wearing a .45 dramatically in a shoulder holster. His eyes were blue and fierce. Paul admired the way he tried to make his H. & S. Company of clerks, cooks and bakers appear to be the spearhead for Carlson's Raiders. He dramatized everything.

The men shuffled together. The Captain glared over their heads at the smoking island of Engebi as if he expected back talk from it.

"We will spend the first five nights on the beach!" he boomed, his voice always ending in an exclamation point.

The clerks and the cooks and the bakers looked at their feet.

The Captain snatched the rifle out of Leon's hands. He held it high above his head, pivoting slowly to glare at his company.

"You will shoot at the enemy!" he explained. "You will shoot at the enemy with this M–1 rifle!"

Headquarters and Service Company was quiet with embarrassment.

The ship's squawk box sounded. "Sweepers, man your brooms! Clean sweep down, fore and aft!"

And as in the dream sequence of a musical play, sailors seemed to rise out of the deck. They were dressed in ragged chambray shirts and silly bell-bottom, faded jeans. Their caps sat jauntily on their heads. In a kind of ballet they began sweeping the deck about the waiting Marines, sweeping as if this were the real job of war and muttering to the Marines, "Watch it, Mac. . . . Hey, mate, how about moving it, huh?" And the Marines became disorganized.

The Marine Captain shook his head as if to clear it and lowered the rifle by the numbers, slapping the stock, the sling, until it was at order arms by his side. Then smartly he brought it back to port arms.

"Whose weapon is this?" he demanded, as if finding it unfit.

"Mine, sir," Leon said meekly.

The Captain thrust his big, shaggy head toward the tiny, brown, hairless Mexican face. "Don't call me sir! This is combat! Marine officers are prime targets to the enemy!"

"Sorry, sir." Leon looked up and smiled sheepishly. "Okay," he added, taking his rifle.

"That's better," the Captain said. Pushing through his men he made his way to the rail, glared down the net at the sea below and the sputtering LCVP's. "Coxswain!" he commanded. "Man your small boat!"

The sailor at the stern of an LCVP cupped one hand to his ear.

"Take us ashore!" the Captain of Marines commanded.

The coxswain's nasal Texas twang drifted up to the Marines on deck. "Ain't got the word yet."

The Captain pushed away from the rail. The men on board could hear the crackling of small-arms fire as the first wave moved up off the beach. The Second Battalion was on the left to take the airfield, the First Battalion on the right to sweep around Skunk

Point. The Third was held in reserve. Paul saw the stern foam of the following second and third waves, as yet to land.

The TBX man had turned on his radio. They heard the static voices from the land as they stood there safely aboard the steel transport. These taut yet casual voices in a background of popping small-arms fire sounded like a bad radio program about World War One. It was impossible to believe when you looked toward that smouldering sunken loaf of land that these voices were coming from there, that people were alive there, alive and with voices. If there were people, were they not some kind of new breed, up from Hell with asbestos skin?

"Frantic to Khaki, Frantic to Khaki," the radio, encased in black rubberized canvas, spoke on the PFC's back. "Am receiving small-arms fire on my left flank. Over."

"Khaki to Frantic. Yeah." A flat voice, almost bored. "I can see your position. Send a BAR man over there and start your move toward the airfield. Over and out."

The platoons talked to their company headquarters, the company headquarters talked to battalion headquarters.

"Khaki to Monitor. Pillbox pinning first platoon down. Request flamethrower. Over."

"Monitor to Khaki. He should be with your team.

Send him up under covering fire of grenades. Over and out."

The Captain did not seem to be interested in these battle reports. He was marching up and down the deck, glaring at his men, shooting glances at the bridge, impatient to be off.

Sailors swept the decks. Other sailors hung around. Some of the Marines had become buddies with the crew of this ship during their eighty-two days aboard. Now these sailors wore different expressions. Just yesterday they had joked, kidded, made deals for souvenirs. Now their eyes were big.

"Hey, Eddie," one of the sailors said to a Marine. "Wanna steak sandwich?" And he pulled a carefully wrapped sandwich out of his shirt.

"Hey," another sailor said, coming up with a large cardboard carton. "You guys got plenty cigarettes? I got small stores to open. How about pogey bait, want some pogey bait?" And before they could answer he began passing out cigarettes and candy.

The squawk box sounded. "Landing team Red, prepare to disembark."

"That's us," Leon said.

"Over the side!" the Captain boomed. He peered down. The coxswain had brought his LCVP up alongside and he and the gunner were hanging onto the bottom of the net. "Keep it taut, sailor!" the Captain yelled.

The Marines, rifles slipping off their shoulders, entrenching tools snagging other packs, began slinging first one leg, then the other over the rail, hanging onto the ropes that made the net.

"Hang onto the vertical, keep your hands off the horizontal rungs!" the Captain yelled, giving the first bit of wise advice for that day. Faces grim, swaying back and forth on the net, the Marines hung on like animals. Paul had seen a Marine freeze on the net during a maneuver and they had had to tie a line around him and club his hands free with a rifle butt.

It was always first things first. Now the net was first and now the net was danger. Concentrate on the net first. If you fell you fell forty feet and got crushed between the side of the ship and the LCVP. The enemy was so remote he was nonexistent. They would face him in time. Now think of nothing else just the net but don't think too deeply or you will freeze on the net. Perhaps this was what made the Marine Corps and combat tolerable. There were so many things to be concerned with before the actual sighting of the enemy, the aiming, the pulling of the trigger. Who did that anyway? They claimed it was less than five per cent.

If it wasn't the net it was always something else. Before the net it was inspection and maneuvers and waiting, the endless standing by. After the net it was getting seasick in the bobbing landing craft and after that it was leaving the landing craft with a kind of joy. And leaving the landing craft there were these thoughts: Is it deep? Is there sharp coral? Will the surf tumble me? Are their mortars on the beach? Still all these things, any one of which could kill you, were bearable in combat for at the very end of this long tunnel the enemy sighted his Nambu. A cut finger, a smashed hand, a broken toe, a gash on the cheek could be serious in civilian life. In combat it was not even noticed.

Marines crowding behind him pushed Paul toward the rail until he and Leon were faced with the rail and the coarse, hairy ropes of the net bound firmly to it.

Leon looked down. "Roark had a long dive."

"Get a move on!" the Captain commanded.

Leon swung a leg over. Neff muttered. Flecks of white foam appeared at the corners of his mouth. His eyes were wild.

The typewriter. The damn typewriter. On his back was the pack and entrenching tool, on his head the helmet, slipping off his right shoulder the M-1, and dangling from his left shoulder the twenty-five-pound black box which was the typewriter. Paul swung one leg over the rail and turned his back to war, to the island, to the enemy, to the objective and the twig-crackling small-arms fire there.

Don't think about the net. His right foot found a

rung and he hoisted his left leg over the rail. He had to lift the typewriter up and over and there it swung, banging against him and the net. The bulky life belt around his middle caught on a rope. A guy above crowded him. Easy, easy. Hang onto the vertical rungs so no one will step on your hands. Hanging away from the ship the net swayed back and forth with the weight of the green Marines. Paul glanced over at Leon but he was already far below, as nimble as a spider monkey on the net.

Strong hands seemed to be pulling him down and away from the net. A Marine's foot clomped on Paul's helmet, jamming it over his eyes. Sixty pounds pulled him down. Don't look down. But he did look down. Heavy and awkward with equipment, Marines swarmed all over the net like flies caught in a spider's web. Stickily they descended.

Now he was halfway down. Now he was over halfway down and the danger of the net and the height of the ship was over. Now came danger number two. Boarding the bobbing LCVP. The LCVP was pale gray with the upturned faces of Marines who had already conquered the net and boarded. It rose and lowered in the gray swells. Drop lightly into the boat, just at the apex of her rise, not as she starts to rise, not as she starts to drop away. Now work down one more rung.

"Jump!" someone yelled.

Paul didn't. He was trapped in the net.

"Watch your feet!" Leon yelled and Paul felt the gunwales of the LCVP softly brush the soles of his shoes. He bent his knees to take up the shock. The guy above stepped on his helmet again. Now his boondockers were on a level with Paul's eyes. Paul stayed. Again the boat rose.

"Jump!" Leon yelled and Paul did. He let go of the net and dropped with a crash to the deck of the LCVP. He felt fingers clutching the fabric of his dungarees, then the flesh of his arms. He swayed. The typewriter pulled him down and he fell with a bang of rifle butt and typewriter to the deck. Deep in its black case the carriage bell of the typewriter rang. Leon pulled him to his feet. He felt like a fallen knight in armor. Another Marine dropped from the sky.

He was in the boat. He looked up at the high gray sides of the transport and the Marines clinging to the net and he looked across the rolling gray sea of the lagoon to the island which indeed, now that he was at water level, seemed to have sunk, finally.

"Boats away!" the Captain sang.

The LCVP sputtered away from the sides of the mother ship, their home for the past eighty-two days, where there were hot chow, dry sacks, a library, movies and small stores to buy ice cream and candy bars. A sailor waved.

"Down in the boat!" the Captain commanded.
Paul sank to his knees as if in prayer. Leon was already leaning comfortably against the starboard bulkhead, chewing on his third breakfast steak.

"You get something in your stomach," he said,
"and you don't get sick."

As if the day, the battle were over, Marines lolled
in the deep dish of the LCVP, their heads over-
weighted by the helmets, rolling back with each
movement, their faces grayish white. The coxswain
pushed full throttle and the Marines looked up to see
the high side of the transport disappear to the stern.
They had been born at sea of this big gray steel
mother and now must face the predators. Above them
the sun was just breaking through to make a hot gauze
bandage of the sky. The coxswain stood at the tiller
in his heroic pose, peering dead ahead at the island.
The gunner leaned casually against the canvas-covered
mounted machine gun. Marines in a deep dish with
sleeping-children heads. Distantly sounded the fire-
crackling of small arms and an occasional dull thud
of a grenade.

Billy, the regimental bartender, seemed to be the
only cheerful one in the boat. He sat relaxed, but
well aware, with his knees up, holding his rifle,
smiling.

Around and around and around they circled in
the rendezvous area. The LCVP's sputtered choking

fumes as they rolled and bobbed in their own wakes. A few Marines were sick.

"In your helmet, son," the Captain advised one green-faced boy. "Keep the decks clean."

They were not allowed to stand up and peer over the side. They sat deep in this bobbing, sputtering, oil-smelling cake pan. Once Billy stood up. The Captain bawled him to the deck.

"What's up?" Paul asked Billy.

"Just going around and around and around with a bunch of other boats."

Then the coxswain got the signal from the command launch and he jammed the throttle forward and squared the boat away. It shot ahead as if it were on a track. The coxswain squatted at the tiller, peering ahead. The gunner removed the canvas from his weapon. The crackle of small-arms fire grew louder. They could hear separate reports. A BAR thudded, *cong cong cong*.

The Captain stood at the scow bow of the boat like a Viking and turned his beefy face to his troops.

"Load and lock!" he commanded.

"Brother," Neff muttered.

The seasick Marines pushed themselves to their knees, fumbled in cartridge belts and bandoliers for clips of ammo. There was a clattering of bolts as they broke open their M–1's and carbines. They inserted the clips, shot the bolts home. They locked their pieces. They stayed in the classic pose, down on one knee, right hand supporting the rifle, its butt to the deck.

Again the Captain turned to his men and as he withdrew his .45 from its shoulder holster in his most dramatic manner commanded: "Fix bayonets and prepare to fight your way out of the boat!"

Neff was breathing heavily. Billy smiled. Leon unsheathed a spotless blade that up until this time had merely been one of the many things that a Marine had to keep in shape for Saturday morning 782 inspection. They fitted the bayonets on the rifle lugs. Paul noticed the coxswain frown at the Marine Captain.

The Bayonet. The psychological weapon. Had it come to this? Infighting. Hand to hand. The acme of combat. They could smell the cordite from the shelling. The yellow coral dust itched in their noses and covered their clothes like a mold.

First with just a whisper below them the LCVP touched bottom, then again harder. The boat lurched, the motor roared. The gunner left his unfired gun and rushed forward to help with the ramp. The Marines crouched, ready. The Captain was at the bow. Good man, he would lead his troops ashore. They were having trouble pushing the ramp down. It stuck. Billy jumped forward to help. The boat was grounded, roaring like a trapped animal. Finally the ramp dropped away out of sight and that end of the boat was open to the enemy, exposing the Marines and their conspiracy.

"Follow me!" The Captain coined a command from World War One. Waving his pistol he crashed out of the boat and into knee-deep water. His Marines followed with fixed bayonets.

They were met with a pastoral scene. Marines leaned against a stack of supplies, eating K rations. Others were in swimming. Three sat on the beach in green skivvies, sunning, smoking, laughing.

This did not in any way affect the Captain. As if they were faced with withering enemy fire he urged his men to keep down, to move forward, to take advantage of cover and concealment, to not bunch up, to move off the beach. His amazed troops obeyed and felt silly as they ran crouched, bayonets glinting, past the sunbathers. The typewriter banged against Paul's knees.

A voice hailed them.

"H. & S.! Over here!" It was Kelton.

As if someone had stuck it there without his knowledge, the Captain stared at the pistol in his big red hand, then jammed it back into the shoulder holster. He confronted Kelton with a glare of hatred and turned to his men.

"Over here," he said. They all straggled over to the large shell hole where Kelton was standing.

The Colonel was already ashore and in the shell hole with his radio man, an orderly, a runner, the intelligence officer, the operations officer and Kelton. The radio crackled. The Colonel was calmly looking at a map. He wore clean dungarees, helmet and unlike the Captain, insignia on his lapels. He was a heavy-set, kindly German, a few years younger than the Captain.

"Headquarters and Service Company ashore, sir!" the Captain reported.

The Colonel looked up and blinked. "Oh, good. Set them up around the CP." He turned immediately to his intelligence officer and they both bent over the map. Kelton stood there grinning. He carried his helmet under his arm like a football player. His hair was wet with sweat and the sweat had caused the black camouflage greasepaint on his face to run.

"Hi, rear echelon," he said to Paul.

"How was it?"

"It still is."

"Dig in, men!" the Captain shouted. "And set up defensive positions."

"Nice bayonet you got there," Kelton said to Paul. Kelton laughed.

Paul removed the bayonet from his rifle and slipped it back into its scabbard. Dazed by the various emotions within him, he looked around. It was as if they had come ashore right after a horrible storm. There was a feeling of the wrath of the elements. Yellow dust hung in the air and it was very quiet where they were, the storm having moved north and past a grove of topless palms. Beyond them, the storm still raged.

"You get dug in and I'll show you around," Kelton said to Paul as if the island were now his very own.

Paul set the typewriter down, stripped off his pack, removed the entrenching tool and began digging his foxhole next to Leon's. It was easy digging in the sand. He dug a passable hole, six and a half feet by three feet by three feet. Leon was digging a mansion, shoring up the sides with coral rocks. Neff said that he wasn't going to dig any damn hole when there were so many shell holes around. Paul put all his gear but the rifle and cartridge belt in his hole, glad to have the typewriter off his back and out of sight. He couldn't imagine himself setting up the typewriter here.

H. & S. Company dug in like a colony of groundhogs and when they were through they sat on the edges of their holes, smoked and listened to the war beyond the trees. Leon dug and dug and dug. Neff sat on his pack and grumbled. Although he was only twenty-five his hair was gray.

"Foolish of me to come ashore," he muttered. "Nothing going on anyway. Lot of work aboard sorting the mail. These guys want their mail they got to let a guy sort it. Makes no difference to me, I never get letters anyway, but guys complain about not getting their mail, well buddies, don't complain to me no more. Not my fault. Should have left me stayed afloat on the command ship to sort it . . ."

Then suddenly, *ping, ping, ping*. Close. Here, right here. H. & S. Company popped into their holes, disappeared into the ground. Neff jumped into Leon's. Leon yelped. Paul raised his head and saw rifle muzzles sticking out of the holes. *Ping, ping, ping.* He couldn't see the spurts of sand from the sniper's slugs. Then most all of H. & S. began firing at once and it was a world of noise and the ting of empty cartridge clips as they left the rifles and flew into the air.

"Knock it off, you bunch of clowns!" Kelton shouted.

The sniper kept firing. Kelton squinted into the palms, then fired a burst from his tommy gun into some fronds. The sniper's fire ceased.

"Didn't see him fall out," Neff said, skeptical.

"They tie themselves in," Kelton said. He turned to Paul. "You ready?"

"Aren't we supposed to stick around?"

"Naw. The companies are damn near to the end of this rock already. Anyway, you're our correspondent, aren't you? Don't you want to see how the battle went?"

Paul found himself walking gingerly as though the whole island would explode if he put his full weight on it. Kelton swung ahead toward the grove of telephone palms and Paul saw his first dead.

A brown full-moon face gazing at the sky with wet painful eyes that looked as if the swollen skin had been neatly slit and ripe olives popped in. A rag-doll body limply falling out of a hole, a body stuffed with straw, for there was straw scattered around. A hole partly covered with corrugated tin. Paul couldn't take his eyes off this dead man, his first dead man, and he thought: Why don't they issue them better uniforms? If they are going to have to die why don't they issue them better uniforms to die in? This greenish uniform was sleazy like play uniforms for kids. With it comes a tin gun and a plastic whistle and a tin badge.

Paul was rooted to the spot, staring at the dead man. Kelton had walked on ahead. Now he paused and turned. The sun was hot. Paul heard a fly. The flies were beginning to arrive. The flies would have a fine time today. This was the day they were waiting for, a heavenly day for flies.

"They're all over like that," Kelton said toward the dead man. "They're dug into this island like ticks in a dog."

"FIRE IN THE HOLD!"

Kelton grabbed Paul and flung him to the ground. Some forty yards away a Marine rolled a grenade across the sand the way you might roll a croquet ball. The Marine flopped. The explosion trembled the ground and shrapnel sang. Paul wondered if he could, all of him could, crawl right up into his helmet.

He looked up finally. Kelton was standing, his tommy gun cradled in his arms. He walked over to the Marines who were now approaching the hole blasted by the grenade. One of them lifted the corrugated tin with his toe and fired a burst into the hole. Paul joined them and saw two more dead blown apart by the grenade, in their little nest like mice with a spilled bag of rice and two perfectly fine bottles of saki.

"I thought the line companies had been all through here," Paul said to Kelton.

"They have. But you can't get them all."

The mop up seemed aimless. The Marines poked about like scavengers in a city dump. But they were part of the island. Paul wondered if he was yet. Yellow-gray dust covered them. They blended in like snakes. Still in the far distance was the sharp snapping of small-arms fire.

"How was the beach?" Paul asked Kelton.

"Not bad. But there was a coconut log revetment where we landed and at first a lot of the guys thought it was going to be another Tarawa. They got down behind the revetment and wanted to dig in." Kelton changed direction and headed toward the beach. "I'll show you."

They moved across the ruined land. It was a soil that Paul had never seen before, a soil that existed only in war, pulverized soil as if the atoms in each grain of sand had split. Paul cupped some in his hands. It was hot, not from the sun, but from the explosions. It was like hot ashes. It was a wonder there was any solid island left. In the yellow air was the smell of this exploded soil, of burning coconut logs, of rubber, and injected into all this, the smell of the dead. It got into your mouth.

They were on the beach now, a little west of where Paul and H. & S. had landed. Kelton pointed out the way the Second Battalion had come ashore, moving up to the O–1 line in boat teams before they regrouped into their own fire squads. Not a building, if there had been buildings, was standing. Not a thing was recognizable except three enemy trucks which were torn from motor to platform, rubber tires smouldering, right-hand steering wheels bent double. What had once been concrete strongholds were but bits of sand and gravel. Wooden water casks were charred and still smoking. Heaps of oil drums had been crushed by bombs and ripped by shrapnel. The palm trees still standing were splintered, grotesque and lifeless. Far away there was the sound of battle.

They heard a click. Kelton pulled Paul to his knees and searched the remaining palm fronds above them. It was quiet where they were. The sun was hot. Far

down the beach they could see the beachmaster supervising the unloading of supplies from the LCVP's.
Then again, this click. And they hit the deck.

They heard someone humming.

"Some of these Japs are goofy," Kelton whispered,
peering up into the palms. "Or drunk on saki or
something."

"Is it coming from the trees?"

They heard the familiar and somehow pleasant
metallic clatter of a rifle bolt being worked back and
forth. "Whoever it is," Kelton said, "he sure ain't
inserting any clip of ammo."

Kelton crawled a few feet to peer over a hummock
of sand, then slowly rose to his feet, looking down
into a shell hole on the beach side of the coconut
log revetment. Paul stood up.

In the shell hole was LeFort, humming to himself
and busily working away on his rifle. The parts were
scattered about in the sand. His oil and thong case
was in his lap. He would pick up a part and carefully
dust it and rub it with a rag, getting all the sand off
it, then toss it back on the sand again and take up
another part. He hummed happily like a child making
mudpies.

"Hey, LeFort," Paul said. "Hey man."

LeFort looked up. His eyes were wide and innocent. "Hi," he said, then bent over his work again.

"Get up, LeFort!" Kelton commanded.

Vigorously LeFort rubbed a rifle part. He looked

up and smiled. "Got sand in my piece. Jammed on me."

"Get up!"

"Soon as I get all the sand out." He placed the bolt mechanism he had just dusted back on the sand.

"Where's your outfit?"

LeFort shrugged.

"You mean you haven't left the beach?" Kelton screamed. "You didn't move up with them?"

LeFort's tone was one of a petulant child's. "How could I? Got sand in my piece. Jammed on me."

"On your feet, LeFort!"

LeFort kept dusting and rubbing.

"On your feet, Sergeant!"

"Soon's I get my rifle together." He blew on the barrel. "Got to get all the sand out." He put the barrel back on the sand and picked up the stock.

"I'll get you another rifle."

"No, no," LeFort cried, looking up at them with anxious eyes. "This is my rifle."

What was so awful was that LeFort sat looking up at them like a dog who thinks he's going to be kicked and is waiting for it.

Paul touched Kelton's sleeve. "C'mon, let's go."

"What?"

"Let him be." Paul pulled Kelton away as LeFort, seeming to have forgotten them, hummed again, busy at his task, dusting, rubbing.

"I'll put him on report!" Kelton grumbled, looking over his shoulder at LeFort.

"You can't do that."

"What do you mean, I can't?"

"The poor guy's cracked up."

"Like hell. He's a deserter, by God, a deserter. He was supposed to lead his squad across the airfield. He let his squad go off without him."

"LeFort should never have been put in charge of that squad."

"But he was." Kelton looked back toward the shell hole. "And it was his job. What if guys got hurt or killed because he didn't do his job?"

They moved onto the airstrip. It was crushed and rolled coral, pockmarked with shell holes. No one was around that they could see. Just the sun on this blinding strip of coral and, beyond the stand of palms to the right, the sound of gunfire.

The two Marines strolled across the airfield, Paul with his rifle at the sling, Kelton cradling his tommy gun, his face dark and furious as he thought about LeFort. Kelton and Paul, a dusty yellow-gray, Kelton's face still black and greasy from the camouflage paint, seemed to be the only Marines on the island. Over to his left across a turquoise patch of water Paul saw an islet, perfect in the sea with its white beach and unviolated palms.

Then close by, just there, the island spoke to them

from the trees in the evenly spaced, feminine *tup tup tup* of a Nambu. Crouching, Kelton ran and Paul after him. But Paul ran awkwardly and not in the rhythm of combat running. Equipment bumped against him, not with him, the way it feels when you are first learning to ride a horse and you are coming down when he is coming up. The helmet bounced crazily on his head. The two water-filled canteens, gurgling, banged against his hips The rifle wanted to slip off his shoulder. Paul felt as if he were coming apart. Ahead of him Kelton ran solidly.

Running crouched and zigzagging across the deserted airfield, Paul felt silly. He didn't see the spurts of slugs in the sand. He didn't hear their song over his head. And again he remembered when as a kid he and the others would play war in the long green Michigan backyards and they would dodge about this way, the way they had seen the World War One soldiers do it in the movies, and sing out like machine guns, "*TATATATATAT*, I got you, you're dead!" To Paul that play war seemed more real now than this war with a real machine gun. Why would they want to be shooting at him? He could understand why those kids in Michigan wanted to shoot at him. They knew him. Here no one knew him.

Tup tup tup. And Kelton suddenly disappeared from sight and then Paul found himself skidding into a shell hole, down down down, safe below ground.

The running exhilarated him and now that he was safe below ground and invisible to machine guns he found himself laughing, almost giggling, at the wonder of it all. He had slid into home plate and was safe.

The laughter was still in him, the grin still on his face as he looked about the shell hole. Besides Kelton there were three other Marines in the hole. Kelton was taking off his helmet and rubbing his sweaty black hair, then removing the package of cigarettes in the webbing of his helmet liner.

One of the Marines was thin and humorous and bareheaded. Another had a radio strapped to his back. The third was busy opening a K ration. The machine gun kept firing for a while, then stopped. Had it really been firing at them? It was all confusing.

"How's it going, Captain?" Kelton asked the Marine without the helmet. The TBX crackled on the radio man's back as if a furious animal were inside it and wanted to get out.

"We've about got this rock secured."

"To the end yet?"

"About a hundred yards to go. How's the Colonel?"

"Happy."

"Good having you along this morning, Kelton. Too bad you didn't stay with us."

"Yeah. Well, you know how it is." Kelton grinned and lighted a cigarette. "We get better chow in regiment."

Paul lay back in the warm shell hole, a hot, gritty womb in this devastated scrap of land, and looked at the faces of the line Marines, the assault troops. Sweat streaked their camouflaged faces like tears. Their bodies seemed feeble, emaciated, certainly not the way you picture Marines. The Captain was slight. He couldn't have weighed over one-thirty. His face was old around his eyes. They talked casually about the landing and the way the battle had gone. Paul was an outsider.

"My boys were sure eager," the Captain was saying. "Wouldn't wait on the O–1 line. Kept going. Fact is they reached the end of the island two hours ago. But when the Colonel came ashore he had me call them back to work with the light tanks."

"Just been on Samoa too long," Kelton said.

"That's right." The Captain nodded. "Well, they know what it's like now." He grinned and poked the third Marine. "Just like your first girl, huh, Eddie?"

Eddie grunted. He was eating the orange cheese out of the dinner K ration. Paul felt out of place, an unwanted guest. He noticed Kelton grinning at him. "Go ahead, Sergeant," Kelton said to him. "Play reporter."

Paul got a nervous grin on his face and couldn't get it off. The Captain was looking at him curiously. Eddie tore the cheese apart with his grimy hands and stuffed his mouth like an animal. Kelton turned to the Captain with a shrug that indicated, we combat people sure have to put up with a lot, don't we? and said, "The Sergeant here is a *combat* correspondent. Maybe you heard about them. PR guys. He writes nice little stories about you for your hometown papers."

"Hey, yeah," Eddie the cheese-eater said. An orange scrap of cheese fell out of his bulging mouth as he spoke. "You get my name in the papers, Sarge?"

"Sure, tell 'em what you did, Eddie," the radio man said. "Tell him how you knocked out all those pillboxes singlehanded, huh?"

Eddie the cheese-eater grinned. He spotted the hunk of cheese that had fallen from his mouth and picked it up, brushing the sand off it. Paul saw that this was going to be difficult.

"What's your outfit?" He got his notebook out.

"Don't tell him," the radio man said. "He works for Tokyo Rose."

Kelton laughed.

"Easy Company," the Captain said.

Paul opened his notebook. They were all watching him. To be saying something Paul said, "Second Bat, huh?"

"Where else do you think it would be?" the radio man said.

Paul ignored this. "You guys had the airfield."

"That's right," the Captain said.

"Just like Tarawa," the radio man said.

THE FIRST DAY 57

Paul looked up quickly. The Captain was sympathetic. He wasn't grinning like the rest. "We thought it was going to be, yes," he said. "When we saw the revetment. But the Marine Corps learned a lot from Tarawa. The Navy gave this island three times the shelling they did Tarawa."

"I wonder if I could have your names?" Paul asked.

"Sure," the cheese-eater said. "Kolowski."

"K . . . o . . . l . . ." Paul said, writing in his notebook.

"o . . . w . . ." the cheese-eater said.

The radio crackled. The Captain sat up. "Eyebrow to Pencil," the radio said. "Am across the island and in swimming."

The cheese-eater was by Paul's side, leaning over his shoulder, looking at the notebook. "s . . . k . . . i," he said.

"Let's go," the Captain said, climbing out of the shell hole.

"What's your hometown?" Paul asked.

"Perth Amboy."

"C'mon," the Captain said, starting off at a run and followed by the radio man. Kolowski clambered up the sides of the shell hole.

"Street address?" Paul called frantically after him.

And the man shouted something over his shoulder that Paul couldn't understand. Paul watched the three of them zigzagging across the airfield and toward the end of the island. He looked down at his notebook, at the one name there, and sighed.

Gnawing on a chocolate bar, Kelton leaned back against the side of the shell hole and grinned. "Ain't war hell," he said.

Paul turned on him. "How come you're always on my back, Kelton?"

" 'Cause it's a safe place to be."

"I'm supposed to do this, you know. It's my job."

"Sure, sure." He stuffed the rest of the bar in his mouth. "Come on, let's get out of here."

No machine gun stitched their steps this time as they crossed the width of the airstrip to the western point of the island where a few coconut trees remained intact and swayed gracefully in the breeze. Here Marines were poking about for souvenirs. They heard shouting coming from the trees.

"Hey! Get 'em! Get 'em!"

Five of the enemy, the first of them Paul had seen alive, were running on their sturdy brown legs out of the grove of palms toward the beach. They wore only loincloths. They splashed into the water and headed for the islet some two hundred yards across the turquoise pass.

All the world was gunfire as the mop-up, souvenir-hunting Marines snapped their rifles to their shoulders and fired at the swimmers. Paul noticed an old Marine gunnery sergeant flick up the ladder rear sight on his .03, check it for distance and windage, then calmly get down on one knee. He raised the rifle, kept his cocked elbow parallel to the deck. He fired.

And cracked open the bolt. The brass tinged out. He shoved the bolt home. Looking up, Paul saw one stationary head in the water.

The gunny fired and Paul saw another swimmer die. And again and again the gunny fired as he had fired for record, wasting no ammo, each slug finding target. He shot them all and now they were just brown bodies in the water being slowly turned around by the current in the pass. The gunny got to his feet, flipped down the ladder sight, opened the compartment in the butt of his .03, took out his oil and thong kit, and began running a patch through the barrel of his rifle.

"The old Marine Corps," Kelton said.

Drawn by the recent death, Paul moved down under the palms where the enemy had been flushed. The other Marines had slung their rifles and continued poking about in spider holes and trench mazes. They had seemed like children, these Japanese, like Polynesian children running to take their morning swim. Paul stood under the rustling palms and watched them float away. They had sprung up from this very ground. This small flat hot island was a tropical iceberg. Way down there in the larger submerged part was a colony of the enemy, crawling about, carrying grains of rice and grenades and occasionally poking their heads out into the sun. Paul turned around. Kelton was gone.

Mop-up groups of Marines drifted by him, proudly carrying their war prizes. Flags and sabers and pistols and rifles. The rifles looked like toys. Their stocks were too yellow to be serious. It was as if the Marines had come only to loot.

Paul wandered over to a half-track. Its driver was sitting up on the gun mount, staring at the small package of four cigarettes that came in K rations as if wondering, since he hadn't smoked before, whether he should start now.

"How did it go?" Paul asked pleasantly.

The driver looked up. "Huh?"

"How was it?"

"How was what?"

"The landing. You know. The battle."

"Okay." Then he looked suspicious. "Why?"

Paul had to get some names. That's what Headquarters Public Relations in Washington wanted. Correctly spelled names and hometown addresses for "Joe Blow" stories. Paul said, "I write stuff for the papers." He took out his notebook. "I wonder if I could have your name and address?"

"Ah hell, I didn't do anything."

"Sure you did. You're here, aren't you?"

"Go ask the line companies. They're the guys to ask."

"I will. But I would like to have your name too."

"I don't want anything about me in the papers. See them other guys. They can give you all the dope."

"How was it when you landed? What did you do?"

"Moved inland."

"Ahead of the troops?"

"Yeah. At first. But then we kept having to go back to the beach to bring up more ammo and juice for the flamethrowers."

"How do you spell your last name?" Paul thought he had worked this in rather cleverly, for the man took the bait.

"M . . . a . . ." he began, then looked down at Paul. "Naw, hey, I don't want my name in the papers."

"Okay." Paul shrugged as if he couldn't care less. He put his notebook and pencil back in his pocket and moved away. He thought the driver would call him back but he didn't.

He was alone. He wandered down the beach on the lagoon side toward his own area. He felt lost, among strangers. He wore their same uniform, carried their same weapon, but they were all strangers to him, living on a different level now, and although the words they spoke were the same words as his they had different shades of meaning. Their smiles were secret, like two people in love. Paul was the third man.

Back near the CP some members of H. & S. were in swimming, others had broken into cases of fruit cocktail and were spooning that out of olive-green cans. Billy, the regimental bartender, sat on the beach, smiling to himself. His dungarees were black with sweat, his pants were ripped.

"Hey, Billy," Paul said. "What were you? Shot out of a gun?"

"Been having myself a time."

"Doing what?"

"With Charley Company."

"How come? You came in our boat."

"Yeah, but as soon as I hit the beach I took off for the line companies." He pointed to the eastern end of the island. "Charley Company over there. Japs were all over the place."

"That's Jenkins, huh?"

"You mean the Captain. Yeah. I knew him when I was tending bar back in Samoa."

"What happened?"

"They were having it rough taking Skunk Point. I just joined a squad and worked with them."

"Think I'll go over there and take a look."

"I'll show you."

Paul followed Billy. Captain Jenkins. Captain, yet. Paul had been pleasantly surprised to see him three months ago on Maui. He liked the feeling but did not admire it, the feeling an enlisted man gets when he sees an old civilian friend who is now an officer. Captain Jenkins. He and Paul had been in the same English seminar four years ago in college, both eager to be writers. Now Jenkins was a captain of Marines, the commanding officer of an assault company which had made a successful landing under fire and which under his command had wiped out a strong enemy pocket.

Captain Jenkins was excited. He was the center of attention in a small knot of officers. His helmet pushed back off his forehead like a running halfback, one hand on his hip, Jenkins was pointing with the other at the various enemy positions on Skunk Point. Paul saw the dead, three, four of them, heaped up behind a Nambu, others in trenches. The scene was unrealistic. Paul and Billy stood back. Billy talked in a rush.

"Queerest people for living in a hole I ever did see. All the naval gunfire or dive bombers in the world couldn't get them out. You got to come in personally and dig them out with grenades and flame-throwers. You got to find them the way monkeys find fleas on each other."

Paul saw the regimental operations officer, a lieutenant colonel, shake Jenkins's hand, squeeze his arm and walk away. The other officers followed. Jenkins stood staring at the ground. He was a small man, with a small sharp face. Paul stepped up.

"Hi, Pat."

Jenkins turned. His thoughts were elsewhere. "Well . . ." Jenkins clapped him on the back. "Well . . ." Paul knew he had forgotten his name.

"I hear you had it pretty rough." He caught Jenkins looking at him trying to figure out who this enlisted man was who had called him by his first name.

"Yeah," Jenkins said. "Around here anyway."

"Skunk Point, huh?" Paul had his notebook out.

"Oh, Paul!" Jenkins said. "How are you, boy?"

"Okay."

"Gettin' any good stories?"

"Yeah. I don't know."

"This was something here. This Skunk Point."

"How did it go?"

"Well, I landed on Beach White One in the assault with Able Company. Baker was in the reserve. First I received only small-arms fire. My objective was this point and I knew I'd be in for it as a destroyer got hit from enemy artillery from this point . . ."

Paul had noticed that certain troop commanders like Jenkins always referred to their company or battalion in the first person. Instead of saying we swept the point or my men swept the point they said, "I swept the point."

"I had a gap on my left flank which A Company was supposed to plug but didn't. That caused me all sorts of hell as the enemy could fire on my exposed flank. I had to throw the reserve platoon in there before I could concentrate on the point."

He walked away with Paul following, writing as best he could. The Captain pointed to the spider trenches. It was all so fresh. The blood so new on the brown faces. "They're crazy, some of these people," Jenkins said looking down at a face by his shoes. "They don't surrender. They'll do the darndest things. Look at them all heaped up behind this one machine gun. Then a couple of times a bunch of them just stood up and started dancing around, waving their arms in the air and yelling, 'Banzai, Marine!' "

Paul had the strange sensation that none of this was real, that Jenkins was reading one of his stories four years ago in English seminar but this time had brought props along to illustrate certain points.

"The only way I could get them out of the holes was to toss in smoke grenades first. That way the exits were marked by the escaping smoke. Then I would send up my flamethrower and a couple of men with grenades to cover the exits while I concentrated on the center target."

"You sure picked up a lot of know-how in two, three hours."

"Yeah, well, you do, you just do." He took off his helmet and rubbed his head. "I mean it was something. It's impossible to describe. I didn't think I would ever be able to do it. I mean I had a company under me." He blinked at Paul. "I lost a few."

"I'm sorry," Paul said.

"Before we hit the beach, when we were bobbing around in the amphtracs, I thought, this is something, this is really something. This is for real. Suddenly I find myself in command of a Marine assault company. Would I ever be able to do it? But you know what?"

Paul looked up from his notebook.

"You just do it. That old Marine Corps saying, a man fights like he trains, it's true. My men had been well trained and they just did it automatically, fire teams of three and four moving up, just the way we had trained on Samoa and Maui, just the way the book says, and it works." He touched the barrel of a Nambu there under the palms, and pitched it over on its back. "Course there's more to it than that."

"I guess," Paul said.

"The dust, the noise, the confusion. It's all so fouled up and then you see a kid you've known for eighteen months with a great big hole where his chest should be. God." He looked at Paul scribbling in his notebook. "I don't know when I'll write about it. Maybe never."

"Yeah, well, this is just hometown stuff, you know."

The radio man came up with the phone outstretched. "Call from Guitar, Captain."

"Okay, thanks. Then I'll see you, Pat," Paul said, moving away. "Thanks." But Captain Jenkins was already busy on the radio.

Paul walked away from this scene of battle. Jenkins was even more a stranger to him than if he had never known him before, as if he had not sat next to him in class for eight months and after class, over a glass of beer, talking about Hemingway and Saroyan and how they were going to write better than that.

Paul saw his first Marine dead. They were all laid out in a peaceful row, sea grape leaves shading their faces like flowers brought to the grave. At first Paul didn't think they were dead, they looked like guys asleep on a boy scout outing, but then from the ash color of their skin Paul knew that they were dead, all of them, over forty Marines in a row side by side, dead. As he passed a handsome first lieutenant Paul knew his life for twenty-three years. Looks like an Easterner. From Hartford, Connecticut. In high school he went out for track, too lanky for football, probably ran the 440. Went to Amherst, was a Deke, looks like a Deke, dated an elegant *Vogue* model type in New York on weekends. Liked to drink beer. Graduated in spring of '41, enlisted in the Marine Corps, went to boot camp on Parris Island, officer

candidates at Quantico, advanced training at Le-
jeune, joined the Twenty-second Marine Regiment
in Samoa, more training and more training and now
here. Here on Engebi, a smouldering coral rock in
the Marshall Islands, atolls that Robert Louis Steven-
son found most lovely. Now here, this first lieutenant.
All those books opened to study all those years. All
those yards run. All that knowledge. All that love
left over. Here now, Lieutenant. You helped give
the Marshalls to the Admiral.

Leon was right in the middle of the unloading
LCVP's in his green skivvies washing his dungarees.
He called to Paul. "It's great. Come on in." Paul stood
on the beach, his unfired rifle at the sling, looking at
the busy boats and Leon scrubbing his dungaree
pants. There was something wrong about it. Looking
toward the sun lowering in the west it was not war-
like. The blue of the lagoon was clean and fresh. The
transports out there could be cruise ships. Down along
the necklace of islets the palm trees were gaily
swinging back and forth in the sea breeze. Paul
stripped to his skivvies and waded in.

Suddenly he found himself laughing and splashing
water like a kid. The dead lay just there, just behind
that low row of sea grapes, and there was intermittent
rifle fire way beyond the trees, but here he and Leon
splashed in the clear blue water of the South Pacific.
Paul swam out a way and turned to tread water

and look back at Beach White One where Jenkins and Charley Company had landed some seven hours before. In the foreground Leon was busy washing. The beachmaster yelled at the unloading boats. The island smoked gently, its fire almost out. He could smell it more sharply now and he dived to the cool bottom and when he surfaced all the war dust was washed from his skin.

Back in the CP Leon strung his wash on a communications wire he had rigged like a clothesline at the foot of his foxhole. His foxhole was a mansion. It was seven feet long and five feet wide and four feet deep. He had made little shelves and niches along the sides and on these he stored his many ditty bags.

The Captain stomped about, frustrated.

"Bandmaster!" he suddenly commanded. "Get your men in defensive positions! Expect a guerrilla attack from the hills!"

"But there are no hills," Paul said to Leon.

"Sounds better with hills." He shook out his jacket and hung it on the wire. "Guerrillas always attack from hills."

Paul noticed an older man, thin and pale, wandering about, bending over to talk to some other Marines. Paul had never seen him before. Probably the bandmaster. "I never knew we had a band," he said.

"They keep to themselves."

His washing hung up, Leon produced a whisk broom from his pack and swept out his foxhole. Cheering came from the command post. The island was secured. All of the companies had reached the beaches on the sea side. Now it only remained to mop up.

Kelton sat down on the edge of Leon's foxhole, spilling sand into it. Leon glared at him. Kelton said, "You and Paul and Neff and me will share a hole tonight."

"Oh, no," Leon said. "After I dug this?"

"We got CP perimeter defense. I got us a nice shell hole all picked out."

Leon looked sad. Kelton said, "That's all right, buddy. Someone will be able to use your hole tonight."

"Yeah. Some officer."

Paul walked over to his foxhole and found another Marine sitting on the edge of it, busily writing in a notebook. Bob Voss, staff sergeant combat correspondent attached to brigade. Bob looked up and grinned. He was a small shy man in his middle twenties. "Found out where you were," he said, touching the black typewriter case with his toe, "by your weapon."

"General Pershing said, 'The deadliest weapon in the world is a United States Marine and his typewriter.'"

"Get any good stories?"

Paul sat on the edge of his foxhole across from Bob. He sighed. "No. God, Bob, I feel like a fool."

"You're being paid to feel like a fool and write about how the others feel like Marines."

"No, I'm not. Every Marine's a fighting man."

"Yeah. That one. They gave us that one in Washington. It was a big pep talk about every Marine a fighting man and all that about the rifle and how we would shoot the rifle and win the war. Then when the Colonel was finished he glared at us and asked, 'Are there any questions?' and White, you remember him, White raises his hand and says, 'Yes, sir. When do we get our raincoats?' "

"Yeah," Paul said. "I know. We're all a bunch of clowns. But is this so important in time of war?"

"Sure it is. Makes everyone feel good. Makes the kid feel good to get his name in the paper. Makes his folks feel better. Helps Marine Recruiting. We got the best PR outfit of all the services. Maybe Air Corps comes close."

"I don't see that it's necessary."

"If you don't, how come you got in PR?"

"I actually don't know now. I always wanted to be a reporter, you know, in civilian life. I had that journalism in college. Then when this combat correspondent deal came up, it just sounded so damn romantic and right for me."

"Say, Paul, not to change the subject, but what's this I hear about some guy going over the side on your ship?"

"That's what he did."

"I hear he got some help."

Paul shrugged. "He wasn't well liked."

"That's the understatement of the day."

"Guys get pretty barbaric in combat."

"But this was before D day."

"Maybe he jumped. I don't know."

"I've heard of guys shooting their own guys but only after they had been on the line a long time. You don't shoot one of your own on the first landing."

"There are some cool cats in this Marine Corps. They got to be that way."

"Yeah, yeah, they're always going on before a landing about shooting some hard-nosed major in the back, but they never do."

"I wouldn't say never."

"You seem to be on the in somehow."

"I'm not. I'm just saying you can't predict what guys will do in combat." He looked at Bob. "I saw a seventeen-year-old kid, hadn't even shaved yet, collecting ears today."

"Ears?"

"Yeah. Japanese ears. He was putting them in a jar of alcohol the corpsman had given him. Held them up proudly for me to see. Said he had fourteen of them so far."

Carrying a Combat Graphic by its once chrome, now olive-green flash gun, Baker, dirty and sweaty, came bobbing up to the two correspondents.

"I thought you guys would be sitting on your butts in headquarters."

"We're the brains, Baker," Voss said. "Often colonels ask us for advice."

"Yeah. You guys got a smoke? I give all mine away."

Paul tossed him his pack. Baker wet the end before putting it between his lips. "I always knew you guys had it easy but I never knew how easy until today."

"We're specialized troops."

"Pictures don't lie. I can't dream up pictures the way you guys can words."

"Now don't give us that one again about one picture being worth a thousand words. Photogs are always giving us that one."

"That's not what I'm talking about even though it is true. What I'm talking about is I got to be right there with the assault boys to get the action shots. You guys can make it all up. You sit on your big butts in the rear echelon and dream up all those corny expressions like, 'I faced withering machine gun fire,' and who is to know differently? But me,

I got to be there right in the middle of that withering machine gun fire to take the pictures otherwise I get fired. And if I take a picture of a TBX man or a guy carrying a carbine or an officer above the rank of captain, headquarters will know I've been hiding my head in the sand with the rest of the rear echelon."

"But what you don't understand, Baker," Voss said, "is that writing those fine phrases such as withering machine gun fire, that takes brains. We are not expendable. We're not just ordinary mechanics like you photogs." Bob was a little guy and his face was round and happy as he faced the harassed Baker.

Baker tossed the cigarette away in disgust. Voss turned back to his notebook. "How do you spell Massachusetts? I can't do it in long hand. I can only spell through my fingers."

"Use my typewriter," Paul said, touching the black box with his toe.

"Too embarrassing."

"How come you didn't bring yours ashore?"

Bob Voss blinked at him. "Didn't you get the word? All us PR guys can go back and forth between the flagship anytime we want. I left my typewriter aboard. Direct radio service to Pearl and then to the States. Civilian correspondents are aboard her. We all file our stories from there." Bob winked at Paul. "Good soft sacks. Excellent chow. We eat with the officers. Why I even got a drink of bourbon last night. Some major thought I was a civilian correspondent and wanted a write-up."

"See what I mean?" Baker said.

"Like tonight," Bob went on. "Nice soft sack, man." He kicked the side of Paul's foxhole. Sand spilled in. "Don't have to sleep in the ground."

"I got guard duty tonight," Paul said.

"You're not supposed to get that, Paul."

"No." Baker laughed. "You're a specialist."

"I mean it, Paul. PR guys aren't supposed to get guard duty, line duty, anything like that."

"Well, I got it. Perimeter defense."

"Just tell them you can't do it. You got your own work to do."

Paul looked at his shoes. "Doesn't seem right."

"What doesn't?"

"Us going back to the flagship. Dry sack, hot chow, out of danger, when all these other guys got to stay here."

"Well, I'm telling you," Bob said. "That's the deal. Everyone else . . ." He waved at the island. "Has got a duty, hasn't he? Well, your duty is to write about it." Bob closed his notebook. "I got eight good stories here. Going back to the flagship now, type them up and give them to the radio operator. That's what you ought to do."

"I didn't get much."

"You got a couple names, didn't you?"

"A couple."

"Then write about them." Bob jammed his note-book back in his pocket and stood up.

"Hey, Sergeant!" Kelton hollered at Paul. "I'll show you your post."

"Tell him, Paul," Bob said. "Tell him you got to go out to the flagship to file your story. That it's orders from the PR officer."

"Is it?"

"Well, not exactly orders, but you got to get your stories in, don't you?" Bob looked at the beach. "There's an LCVP ready to go out now. Better hurry." He trotted down toward the beach, yelling at the coxswain of the LCVP.

Baker moved away in his curious waddle. "Guess I'll take some scenic shots. You know, curving palms, naked Marines."

Paul walked over to Kelton. Paul thought about telling Kelton that he should go out to the flagship, but when he saw that fixed smirk on Kelton's face he knew that he couldn't. Paul followed Kelton away from the CP and to a shell hole in the middle of the cleared area. Some fifty yards ahead was the second stand of splintered palms. Behind them was the CP and the H. & S. Company area.

"You and Leon and Neff and me will take this post. Has a good command. Be sure to get to it before dark."

Paul was troubled. He knew Bob Voss was right. Or did he know? He should write a couple of stories, radio them in. That was his job. But how could he? Wasn't guard duty in combat more important than typing? And how Kelton would hoot with derision when he told him. "Scared of the dark, Sergeant?" he would ask. Paul could just hear him.

Paul walked back to Leon's foxhole. Leon was as busy as a new bride arranging his K rations. Each man had been issued enough to last a day. Dinner, Supper and Breakfast and they came in boxes the size of Cracker Jack boxes. The D or Dinner ration was the best because of the can of fine yellow cheese and the chocolate bar. This bar, shaped like a small gold ingot, was heavy and firm and rich. A Marine could exist on this bar alone. Somehow Leon had managed to get three Dinner rations. Now he sat on the edge of his foxhole before the tiny collapsible stove. He had lighted the white heat tablet and was brewing powdered soup. Small pleasures made Leon happy. He hummed and smiled as he fussed in his kitchen.

Paul lighted a heat tab. It flamed a wet blue. He poured half a canteen of water and set it on the little stove. Leon, mouse-dainty, nibbled his yellow cheese and made a face as Paul opened his tin of potted meat that came with the Supper ration. Beyond them still was the sporadic crackling of rifle fire and an occasional dull thud of a grenade as the line companies continued to rout the enemy from spider holes and out of the palm fronds.

Neff came crashing up to Paul and Leon with a can of filched fruit cocktail and stabbed it open crudely with his combat knife. Neff, grinning, bearded, sweaty, his eyes afire as if he had been talking with the devil, Neff slurped the syrupy bits of pineapple and peach noisily. Leon glanced at him with distaste.

The water was boiling in Paul's canteen cup. He tore open the metallic envelope of powdered coffee and dumped it in the water and stirred it. He waited a minute. He tried to sip it. The rim burned his lips. He set the cup down and put the tiny can of potted meat on the stove. He tried the coffee again. As he knew it would it still burned his lips. Canteen cups. It was a big deal in the Marine Corps, always had been, always would be, to be salty "old Corps." Paul's canteen cup was old Corps. Its rim was solid, round, shiny, spun aluminum. He wouldn't part with it for the world. New issue was a better cup, that is at least you could drink from it. In the old issue cup the coffee was cold before the rim cooled off enough so that it would not burn your lips. But the old cup was like the felt campaign hats and the square-ended field scarfs and the delicate emblems. They showed that you had time in the Marine Corps. That you were an old salt. This was important.

Paul spooned some of the coffee with the large Marine Corps spoon. The thoughts of the night ahead bound his stomach tightly and the coffee splashed into it like water onto rocks. He thought of Bob Voss now safe and warm and full of good chow aboard the flagship, steel plates on all sides of him. Why couldn't he, Paul, be there? What was he scared of? The war? Or Kelton? The potted meat sputtered over the heat tab. It smelled good. Using his combat knife as a spatula Paul lifted the can off and began to eat. It was hot, too hot, but it tasted good.

4

Night

K ELTON APPEARED above them, a tall silhouette against the gray sky. "Check your combat knife," Kelton said. "And fix bayonets."

"Fix bayonets," Neff said. "You kidding? That's the second time we heard that today."

"Fix bayonets," Kelton ordered.

He led the three Marines to the shell hole he had showed Paul earlier. "You got time for one more butt," he said as they dropped into the hole and leaned back against the warm sand. But before they had a chance to light up he said, "Now I want you men to study this terrain in front of us. We got about fifty yards of nothing but sand and rubble, then that grove of palms. If they come, they'll come out of the palms. Memorize what you see so that later on when it gets dark you won't think that lump of sand there is a Jap."

Neff had cracked open his rifle and was blowing

on the clip of ammo. Kelton frowned. "Above all, maintain fire discipline. I don't want any indiscriminate firing. When you see something move, don't fire at it. Wait until it gets close, make sure, then use your bayonet or knife."

With trembling fingers Neff used three matches to light a cigarette.

Kelton went on. "None of our men will be moving around tonight. We have a third relief of guards behind us in the CP but they will be kept in reserve, just in case the enemy does decide to counterattack. It would be too dangerous to post them in darkness. So just lie low and wait and watch."

The light faded from this scrap of land. A smell of coolness was in the air. A fresh breeze was coming off the sea directly ahead of them and it did not carry with it the foul smell of death. It was a clean, fresh sea smell as if the war had never been. Paul peered out the shell hole at the grove of palms ahead, then back toward the CP. The only man visible was a message-center runner dodging foxholes and shell holes, and then he disappeared, plop, as quick as that. Now no one was visible. They were all dug into the ground. The island appeared to be deserted. It was very quiet.

"Smoking lamp is now out," Kelton announced. "Me and Leon will take the first watch."

It was dark. It was night. It was black. Paul curled

into the womb of the shell hole. How could it be possible that a mere hole in the ground could provide such luxury?

Although Kelton and Leon had the first watch from eight until twelve and were on their bellies, lizard-like, to peer over the rim of the shell hole, this did not mean that the two other Marines were able to relax. It was too early for sleep. Paul and Neff crept up alongside Kelton and Leon. It was a fortunate watch for now instead of two pairs of eyes four peered into the darkness ahead. The black night. The unknown came out now. Paul remembered the nights of his childhood that were filled with shapes of the unknown on the ceiling of his bedroom. There were claws and warty hands reaching for him and he would duck under the covers and they would go away. If he would hide his head under his poncho now, would the war go away?

The night was cool and dark. Eight eyes peered up over the rim of the shell hole. But how many other eyes were watching the night? Who would think that such a casually tossed scrap of land in the blue Pacific would someday hold so many wary eyes? Paul stared into the darkness. His eyes felt sandy.

Kelton poked him. "You and Neff better rest your eyes otherwise you won't be any good on your watch."

Paul and Neff rolled back into the hole. Neff bit a cigarette in half and chewed it. He was breathing heavily. He spit. "Not bad." He grinned at Paul.

Then they heard firing beyond the palms. Paul scrambled back up to the rim of the hole again. "Nambu," Kelton whispered. They couldn't see anything. It was as if the island stuttered in the night to complain of the Marines on its back.

The way tree frogs answer each other at night, other weapons now answered the Nambu. *Cong cong cong* of a BAR. Thud of a grenade. The night became gregarious. Still Paul could not see anything. "To relax your eyes," Kelton said, "blink them and hold the blink. But you're not on watch. Get back down there."

The firing stopped as suddenly as it had begun. Neff spat out strands of tobacco. Curled up in the fetal position at the bottom of a shell hole on a South Pacific island Paul looked up at the night carelessly strewn with stars and thought, as he would again, as would every man involved in this war, "What am I doing here?"

Ducking their heads under the covers so that the night monsters would go away, Paul and Neff curled in the shell hole, turning their backs on war. If they were going to have to be killed, they didn't want to see it done. Hit me here, right here in the back of the head, but I don't want to see you do it. Paul's grip relaxed on the stock of his rifle. He felt lazy, bored.

Night became day. A weird, unholy day of a manufactured, blue-white, ghastly light. It was a trick. God had sent a small death sun into the sky to trick them into thinking it was day and it wasn't at all. Then Paul heard the factory of this sun, first the cough of a mortar, then the soft pop as it blossomed into being above them. He moved up past the hanging limp feet of Kelton and stared at the sizzling flare.

The swinging flare caused the shadows to move in the fifty yards of terrain between them and the grove of shattered palms. Instinctively Paul reached for his rifle. His hand closed around the stock the way primitive man's closed around a club. The shadows moved in creeping blots, flowing across the floor of this island to drown them with their hot and inky breaths. Then he heard the screaming and he gasped.

Kelton grunted. The faraway screaming came toward them in waves. A BAR spoke. More screams in the night, tattered red ribbons of bloody screams. A grenade belched its one ugly word. The screaming stopped. Then a silence so thick you could squeeze it in your hands and it would come oozing out between your fingers like mud. The last swinging flare sizzled out. The night was as black as a velvet hood over their heads. Paul let himself slip to the bottom of the shell hole to curl up again, comforted by the nearness of Neff. But it seemed as soon as he had done so someone was roughly shaking his shoulder. "Your watch," Kelton spat into his ear.

Now just two pairs of rusty eyes were responsible for the safety of this hole of a home and what lay behind it. Suddenly this responsibility became too much to bear for Paul and with this feeling came one of lassitude and utter helplessness. If it were too much to bear, then why bear it? Why not get this whole thing over with and let the shadows creep. When pressure becomes unrelenting, lethargy follows. Paul felt sleepy. He just wanted to sleep. Funny, he had been wide awake in the bottom of the shell hole when Kelton and Leon were on watch.

The cough. The soft pop. The swinging flare. A phony brilliant day. His breath was high in his lungs and when he heard its sizzle the noise seemed to be searing his face. Paul watched the shadows move. He turned to look back into the shell hole. Kelton and Leon, curled like babies in the bottom of the hole, were already fast asleep.

Damn them! Paul felt the anger choking him. Damn them anyway! This was unfair. How did they dare sleep? All through their watch he and Neff had been awake in case they needed help. He felt like kicking Kelton awake. Who did he think he was to sleep with a war going on? Paul turned to the white sizzling view in front of his eyes, his hands clumsy and sweaty on the stock of his rifle, his bayonet slantwise toward the broken trees. Beside him Neff kept making little gasps in his throat. Neff raised his rifle. Dumbly Paul blinked at him, then squinted at the shadows.

"See something?" he whispered.

"Thought I did."

Paul had accepted the fact that there was to be no firing. If they wanted fire discipline, then by God they'd get it. He wouldn't fire at all, not at all. Even if there were a Banzai charge he wouldn't fire. He'd show them. He made his mind up not to fire, ever. He had locked his piece and his finger rested on and not in the trigger guard. The embarrassment of firing now when there was nothing to fire at, the jeering faces of his comrades in the sunlight when they yelled, *trigger-happy!* at him, that was far worse than not firing and being killed as a result.

Paul peered into the swinging light of the flare. It winked once, then popped itself out so that he could see the orange glow of coal and his eyes remembered the whiteness. Fifty yards of humps before him. Had Neff seen anything? His memory of that afternoon of the spider holes and underground nests did not help. They were in the ground like animals. Who was to know when or where they would appear again? One could be dug in beneath them right here. First there would be a little sifting of sand as he dug for the surface, then he would pop his head out right in the middle of them all, at first grinning, then snarling and snapping like a mad dog.

Paul heard a noise. A new noise. It hammered in his ears even though it was a small noise. His body became stone-cold. "Neff!" he inhaled. Neff turned. They listened. A scratching in the sand. Forcing himself, Paul peered in the direction of the noise. He saw nothing. Now why didn't they shoot off another flare? That was the trouble. When you didn't need light, when light was the last thing in the world you wanted, they gave it to you in suns. But now when you needed it, where was it? Perhaps it was better this way. He didn't want to see the face of the thing that would kill him.

Closer came the fumbling, fussing noise. "Kelton, Kelton!" Paul whispered urgently, tapping Kelton's helmet with his knuckles.

Kelton snapped awake and moved smoothly up alongside Paul. His machete was unsheathed and held easily in his right hand.

"Listen!" Paul whispered.

Scratching, fumbling, searching. Three Marines taut against the slope of the shell hole looking into the blackness, alert and listening, fists clenched on weapons.

Then Paul felt Kelton relax. Kelton chuckled. He reached out with his machete and touched something, then scooped it up and brought it into the shell hole before tossing it away. "Good man," Kelton said. "A land crab." Kelton slipped back down into the hole. Paul felt the warmth in his face. Then he muttered. Well by God next time he'd let a Jap come right on past him and jump down on Kelton.

Another flare. Of course. When they didn't need it. And with the flare came the night voices. Clearly now Paul heard, "Banzai, Marine!" He searched the trees ahead but could see nothing. "Banzai!" And the crackle and cong of rifle fire and the thuds of grenades. "Banzai!" they screamed beyond the trees and Paul wished he could scream with them, could get the foul air out of his body by screaming.

Just before the flare sizzled out he heard the flat, blunt report of a .45 behind him in the direction of the CP. Then a yelp, cursing, moaning. Finally it was quiet again.

The night was as long as a lifetime. Neff, chewing cigarettes, kept looking at his watch.

"What time is it?" Paul would ask.

"One-twenty."

And after what seemed like an hour later he would ask again. "What time is it?"

"One-twenty-five."

The night passed with each second noted. Then finally the miracle. The night did have an end. The east grayed and it was day. The evil shadows they had been staring at all night became innocent lumps and logs. How silly it had been to be scared. What a monster darkness is.

It was morning for sure. Paul looked behind him and saw the helmets of other Marines out of their holes and he saw their grinning faces. There was a great joy among them. They had made it. It was day and day was lovely. A cigarette now was a banquet. The long night was over and they could smoke. They had done nothing extraordinary, just what thousands did every night in every combat zone, stood guard, and like all the others, they were overjoyed to see the morning light.

The sun nearing the sea horizon turned the gray of the island to color. Green, yellow, brown, beige. The word passed from hole to hole. Remember the shot and a scream in the CP last night? Jones, a company runner, had been shot. He had been moving about at night and he had been shot by one of his own men who thought he was the enemy. Who did it? No one asked.

As the sun rested on the horizon, getting ready to leap free of the sea world, the round notes of a bugle sounded. With the others Paul jumped to his feet and stood at attention. There on a bamboo pole in front of the CP the colors were being run up and the field music was playing attention to colors on a captured enemy bugle. Paul felt the lump rise in his chest at the sound of the bugle, at the sight of the flag.

5

The Second Day

ALTHOUGH the island had been called secured the
afternoon before the importance of mop up was made
clear to them that morning. Most of the Marines
were squatting over their heat tabs and cups of warm-
ing water when suddenly not ten yards from the
CP appeared a Japanese wearing a loincloth and
swinging a bottle of saki and singing. The CP at
this time held not only the regimental commander
but the Brigadier General as well, plus a handful of
staff officers.

He didn't get far. The regimental interpreter kept
screaming at the Marines to hold their fire, he wanted
the man to question, but it was too late. The enemy
was felled on the spot and a good thing he was for
the bulge in his loincloth turned out to be a grenade.

Paul knew what he should do. He should set up
his typewriter on the rim of the foxhole and turn
out some copy. That was his job in this operation

and he'd better get on it. The black box was in his lap and he was about to open it when he heard Kelton's voice behind him.

"Going to write about battling with a land crab, Sergeant?"

Paul glared up into the jeering face. He set the typewriter down. "I was just getting the dirt off it."

The sun was hot and again the dust was in the air from the boondockers of the Marines combing the island and firing into spider holes and palm fronds, rolling grenades and screaming, "FIRE IN THE HOLD!"

Paul slung his rifle and, trying to look as if he were off on some important errand, marched off down the beach past the growing stacks of supplies to where the Second Battalion had landed the day before. There he found a company of gray-green dusty victors, their battle over, joking, waiting on the beach for the LCVP's to take them back out to the transports.

Even though he wore the same dusty dungarees and leggings, the same boondockers and helmet, carried the same rifle, Paul found it difficult to join them. A civilian couldn't tell Paul from the assault troops, but they could.

To the victors belong the spoils and Paul stood just outside this group on the other side of the invisible fence and watched them eating the stolen cans of fruit cocktail and holding up the souvenirs of war.

"Hey, look, this guy had a girl," one of them said, going through a wallet.

"Well, I'll be damned," another said in amazement, looking at the snapshot.

One of the Marines, a gunnery sergeant, noticed Paul. "What can I do for you, Sarge?"

Paul was glad of the opening. He smiled. He thought it best to plunge right in. "Well, see I'm a correspondent and I . . ."

"A what?" The gunny moved closer to Paul.

"Well, I . . ."

The gunny was smiling. He pointed to one ear. "Don't hear so good. Mortar burst about an inch from that ear last night."

Paul nodded and said in a louder voice so that some of the others turned to look. "I write stuff about Marines overseas, in combat and all, for their hometown papers."

"Say that's pretty good," the gunny said, showing interest. He was a young-looking Marine for a gunnery sergeant, with the hard, classic, football jaw. His face was clean and freshly shaved.

"I was just wondering if I could get some stories from the men in your company."

The gunny smiled. "I'd say you could get plenty." He turned to the Marines lolling on the sand and leaning up against the shattered palms. "Hey, you guys, listen a minute." He nodded to Paul. "The

Sergeant here's a correspondent. Writes stuff for the newspapers. You got any stories for him he could write up?"

Paul felt their eyes on him going over him carefully, some curious, some suspicious, some without interest. Some laughed, then fell silent.

"Well, come on," the gunny said. "That's all you could talk about a minute ago."

"Anything unusual happen yesterday and last night?" Paul asked. Right after he said it he knew it was a bad choice of words.

"Unusual, yeah," one of them said. "That's what it was all right, unusual."

They snickered.

Paul crouched down. "What I meant was . . ." He smiled. "Well. What happened?"

"Tell him about Flores," one of them said excitedly.

"Yeah, tell him about Flores."

"Huggins too. Don't forget Huggins."

Paul slipped the notebook out of his pocket. They were all enthusiastic about their buddies and this enthusiasm came from the fact that the battle was over for the time being and they were waiting for the LCVP's to take them out to the mother ship and small stores and clean sacks safely behind steel bulkheads.

"The pineapple kid," the gunny said. "That's what we called Flores."

"That guy had a bag of grenades."

"Yeah, he carried them around like groceries."

"Where is he now?" Paul asked.

"He got hit. But not bad. Stateside wound, I bet."

"How about the way Barton fixed him up?"

"Yeah, that Barton."

"That corpsman turned out to be okay."

"What'd he do?"

"Who, Barton?"

"Yeah, but first, Flores. What did Flores do?"

"He was all over the place with his grenades," the gunny said.

"He planted them," another Marine said. "The way you plant flowers."

The gunny laughed. "What he'd do is he'd spot, and that guy had the sharpest eyes, a spider hole, some sand sifting or something and he'd know it was an emplacement and then he'd just trot up there, he never threw grenades, he'd trot up there, reach in his bag, pick a grenade, pull the pin and as if the grenade were an orange he'd just place it by the hole and then casually trot back and hit the deck briefly while the grenade went off."

"I bet he used a gross of grenades."

"The pineapple kid, huh?" Paul wrote this in his notebook.

"That guy should have been a gangster in Chicago."

"If he wasn't I bet he will be."

"He and old Huggins had themselves a ball once they got squared away."

"What about Huggins?" Paul asked.

"He was funny. It was last night, see, and we were all dug in and it was scary as hell with the Japs yelling at us and those flares and someone slips into Huggins's hole with him and at first he thought it was Flores but then he sees it's a Jap and Huggins says without thinking, 'Take off, Mac,' like that and the Jap does and then Huggins realizes who it was and what he said and so he yells, 'Hey, Mac, wait a minute,' and he jumps up as the Jap turns and guts him with his bayonet."

"Where did you guys hit the beach?" Paul asked the gunny.

The gunny pushed himself up a little and looked down the beach and toward the lagoon. "About in here, yeah right about in here."

"How did the landing go?"

The gunny grinned. He nodded to a sullen-looking Marine slouched up against a palm tree. "Terry over there, I guess, was the first Marine on this rock, weren't you, Terry?" Terry didn't answer. "Yeah," the gunny said. "It was funny as hell. Terry crashes ashore and then he stops and looks around and up and down the beach and there he was standing all alone. He looked like a kid lost from his mother in a department store." Terry snorted. "But he wasn't alone for long."

"Then you guys moved up on the airfield, huh?"

"Yeah. That was our objective. At first you know, I guess it was like buck fever or something. We were only receiving small-arms fire and couldn't tell where it was coming from. I suppose you could say we were scared, sure we were, but it was more like buck fever too or whatever you want to call it. Then we saw our first Jap. He was firing at us from a spider hole just off the airstrip. Kelton began his move then and . . ."

"Kelton?" Paul interrupted.

"Yeah. He's from regiment. Two section. Know him?"

"I know him."

"Well when he moved forward it sort of broke the ice with the other guys and they turned into a bunch of hounds closing in on a cornered fox. They ran forward with fixed bayonets all excited and yelling, 'Hoppo, hoppo!' "

"What do you mean by that?"

"Hop head. Half of them are hopped up, I believe. Either that or drunk on saki and all crazy from the naval gunfire. After that first Jap the guys calmed down, the buck fever disappeared and they settled down to the job."

"You know Kelton pretty well?"

The gunny looked at him. "Not too well. Knew he'd been on the 'Canal. He's a wild man."

"He's pretty good, huh?"

"I would say he was a natural. I don't know how he'd hold up in the peacetime Marine Corps, but he was made for the wartime Marine Corps. You ever hear about him on the 'Canal?"

"No."

"Got it from a buddy of mine who was with the First. That Kelton was all over the place. A natural killer. Smooth. He was with Barney Ross when they heaped up all those Japs before the machine gun. My buddy says Kelton is best hand to hand. Likes it. Knows all that judo stuff. Likes to get his hands on the guy personally. The General heard about Kelton and wanted him as his bodyguard but Kelton would have no part of it." The gunny grinned. "Probably just as well. Kelton would probably end up sticking the General. No telling what he would do, according to my buddy, when he got in the mood and he always seemed to be in the mood."

Paul nodded.

"Hey, Sarge." A Marine tugged Paul's sleeve. "You wanna hear about Barton?"

"Yes," Paul said. "What about Barton?"

"Old Doc was great. He . . ."

But he was interrupted by the First Sergeant. "All right, you people, the boats are here. Let's get off this stinking rock."

The Marines cheered and jumped up, shouldering

into packs. The gunny clapped Paul on the shoulder as he started to follow the men to the waiting LCVP's. "See you, Sarge."

Looking at his notebook Paul said hastily, "How do you spell Flores?"

"Like it sounds."

Paul yelled after him, "You wouldn't know his hometown address, would you?"

"Flores was from New Jersey some place. Dago kid."

Paul stood there on the rim of the shell hole and watched them moving down the beach to board the LCVP's. Why couldn't he have been Flores, who had showed his salt and now could relax? Why couldn't he have been Terry, the first man on the beach? Why couldn't he have been any of them and had it over with now? Why couldn't he have been Kelton? No, not Kelton. Maybe Kelton. One man like Kelton to taint a company of Marines could win the war in double time. The professional killer. That's what they needed in time of war.

Paul walked back to the CP. The company Captain was shouting orders. "Police the area! Pick up your brass!" The H. & S. Marines poked listlessly about in the hot sun. In one shell hole, bareheaded, looking at his hands, sat LeFort. Another Marine with his rifle in his lap sat opposite him.

"Hi, LeFort," Paul said.

LeFort looked up with dead eyes.

"How did it go?"

LeFort bowed his head.

"You okay?" Paul asked.

LeFort nodded. "Sure I'm okay." He blinked innocently at Paul. "Just got some sand in my rifle is all."

"I know."

LeFort looked suspicious. "You know? How come you know?"

"I saw you yesterday, remember?"

LeFort kept glaring at him.

"When you were in the shell hole. Cleaning your rifle."

"Oh yeah. I had to clean it. You saw how sandy it was, didn't you?"

Paul nodded.

"Well I had to clean it then, didn't I? Can't fire a rifle with sand in it."

"LeFort. Did you see the doc?"

"The doc? What for?"

"I think you ought to go see the doc."

"Hey, Sarge," the guard said to Paul. "No talking to the prisoner, huh?"

"Okay," Paul said. He turned away, then back. "LeFort, tell them you want to go see the doc."

Paul walked toward his foxhole. So Kelton had turned in LeFort for desertion after all. Paul felt sick at heart for LeFort. Maybe he ought to tell the doc about LeFort. The guy cracked up. That's what happened. It wasn't his fault. He just cracked up. But at least now LeFort knew where he stood. At least that thought, What will I do under fire? was out of his mind. Flores and the others could say to themselves, I took it. I can take it. LeFort could say, I couldn't. I can't. But Paul. Paul could say nothing. All he had done was battle with a land crab.

Paul sat on the edge of his foxhole and stared at the notes he had made. The pineapple kid. He had to get Flores's and Huggins's and Terry's full names and addresses. He noticed Kelton getting into his gear.

"What's up?"

"Army's having a rough time on Eniwetok Island. Third Bat's been called in to help them."

"Yeah?"

"Damn dogfaces won't move. They're still on the beach waiting for artillery and air support."

"That's the way they been trained."

"No way to fight an atoll war. The Admiral wants this entire Eniwetok atoll secured as fast as possible. That way he can bring his planes in."

"You going down there?"

"Eniwetok? Sure. It'll be fun to run through those dogfaces."

"We got Parry to go yet."

"I'll be back by then."

Leon ambled up. "Hey, Kelton, we get another battle star for Parry?"

"Naw, what the hell."

"Why not? It's another landing, isn't it? It's another battle."

"What of it? This is one operation, this Marshalls operation. No matter how many islands we land on and take."

"Doesn't seem fair," Leon said. "Air Corps guys get another oak leaf cluster every time they walk by their planes."

Kelton was all geared up, pack and entrenching tool on his back, helmet on his head, tommy gun slung over his right shoulder. He turned to Paul. "I won't ask you if you want to come along 'cause I know you don't." He yelled at the coxswain of a waiting LCVP on the beach. "So long, rear echelon," he said to Paul. "Watch out for land crabs." He ran down to the boat.

"That guy's crazy," Leon said. "He's asking for it."

"Yeah," Paul said as he watched Kelton running up the ramp of the LCVP and the ramp closing and the gray scow backing off the beach.

Leon handed Paul half of a fruit bar. "Have some pressed flies."

Paul chewed on the black, dried fruit. "You hear about Kelton on the 'Canal?"

"Nope. And don't care if I ever do."

"From what they say he was a one-man Marine Corps."

"I wish that were true. Then they'd let me go Stateside."

"I wouldn't be surprised if he didn't have a little tussle with Roark that night."

"Oh, he threw him over the side all right."

Paul turned to Leon. "You think so?"

"I think so. I don't know so."

"Headquarters and Service Company!" the Captain shouted. "Prepare to move out."

"Oh, man. Here we go. Off this stinking rock."

The Marines elbowed into their packs, clapped their helmets on their heads and shouldered the rifles few had fired. Even the members of H. & S. Company carried souvenirs of war, flags and rifles they had found or, perhaps nearer the truth, bartered for with the assault troops. H. & S. Company looked as battle weary as the assault troops. But there was a difference in the eyes. In the eyes of the assault troops there was a deepness, a sureness. H. & S. Company's eyes still fluttered.

With equipment clanking the Marines left their foxholes. Leon turned to look longingly at his shored-up mansion with its little shelves. They moved on down to the beach. Here green garrison troops were stepping out of the LCVP's and looking warily about them. They were freshly shaven and dressed in clean dungarees. Now it was H. & S.'s turn to be salty. The line companies could be salty with H. & S. for not landing in the first wave, now H. & S. could be salty with the garrison troops for not being on the island when the battle was on.

"You'll be sorry," H. & S. shouted at them in the old boot camp jibe. "You'll be sorry!"

"Look smart!" their Captain bawled at them.

H. & S. Company boarded the sputtering LCVP's and roared out into the lagoon. There at the sleek steel skin of their transport they again met with the nets but now they must go up them instead of down. But with fond memories of their six by two racks and hot chow they clambered up the nets like monkeys. Paul never felt the weight of his pack and rifle, never felt the typewriter banging against his knees.

Back aboard the sailors greeted them as heroes, clapping their backs, looking for friends, handing out ice cream and candy bars, helping to carry packs and weapons. But one sailor, a salty boatswain's mate who had been a coxswain at Tarawa, was sour.

"You guys had it easy. You guys walked ashore. The Marshalls are a pushover compared to the Gilberts. I oughta know. I was both places."

Some Marines fell silent, if only briefly, for they knew it was true. Tarawa had been rough and now Engebi was a disappointment because it hadn't been.

When the last Marine was hauled over the nets, they were pulled up and aboard and the voice came over the squawk box: "Special sea and anchor detail report to your station." The hook was lifted and with the other ships the big gray transport began to turn on the glassy waters of the lagoon and to glide effortlessly toward the south and the next beach-head.

Paul stayed by the rail and looked at the ruined scrap of land he had just left, still smoking, a ragged disc with a now richer soil from the spilled blood. From this far out in the lagoon Paul could hear the bulldozers of the Seabees working on the air strip, and digging the graves.

As the ship turned he looked down the rail. That way lay Parry, and beyond Parry was long Eniwetok Island where Kelton and units of the Third Battalion were moving in to give a hand to the Army and secure the island for the Admiral. Now directly before him were the lovely coral islets. Their palm trees were as graceful as young girls in a ballet class, nodding their heads to him in the breeze. Once Engebi had been like this.

Down below, Paul set up his typewriter in a corner of the hold and wrote a two-page piece about

Flores, the pineapple kid, but he didn't like it. It was flat and thin. He wished he had actually seen Flores doing these things. Still he should be able to write it. That's what reporters did. They reported the disasters without actually becoming involved in them. Reporters were outsiders trying to get inside. Somehow he couldn't.

It was dark when he again went topside. As they neared Parry in the darkness, the ship slowed. Before maps and papers had been found on Engebi, Parry was thought to be deserted. Because of its airfield Engebi was picked to be the enemy stronghold of Eniwetok Atoll. Now they had discovered that it was Parry. Imperial Marines were her garrison troops. The Admiral's headquarters was there.

Who can see a colony of ants underground? That was why not much of anything had been seen in the aerial photographs of Parry. If it had been, this convoy certainly would not have made the reef entrance at Parry. The grand ships had passed within a hundred yards of Parry's northern tip. A coastal gun could have sunk them as easily as bathtub toys. Then why hadn't it? For some inscrutable reason the enemy had chosen to remain hidden underground and quiet.

Paul heard the rattle of the anchor chain. They were off Parry. The searchlight of a destroyer was roving about the banana-shaped island, hesitant, finally centering. Then there was a flash and another flash and another and sometimes Paul could see the orange-red dot of the projectile slowly passing the length of the beam of light. Fire splashed as the shell hit, but sometimes this same red dot reemerged in a ricochet and winked out finally in the darkness beyond the beam, beyond the island and far out to sea. Count to twenty-eight, all the time forming the boom on your lips, and then, WHAM!

The day after tomorrow they would see what the shelling had done.

6

Parry

THIS MORNING there was no steak for breakfast. It was as if the fuss and attention of opening night were over. Now it was a bore to the mess sergeant and his messmen to pamper the troops. This morning they were served warm, canned grapefruit juice, cold cuts and coffee.

This morning as they waited for the call to the nets they sweated a different sweat and their dungarees smelled of war. This morning it didn't seem fair. How much could they take? Two landings in four days. The beachheads were the toughest part always. And their Third Bat had to go down to help the Army. Talk about Tarawa. Wasn't this rougher? Two landings in four days. That just wasn't fair.

But deep down inside every man he felt proud. The Twenty-second Marines, now finally blooded, were called upon to do something special. They could be trusted to do the job.

Paul had decided not to take the typewriter in with him. He hadn't used it on Engebi, had he? Making this decision made him feel giddy. He sat bunched up with the rest in the forward part of the hold and smiled about it. He was like them now. He carried no badge of rear echelon identification. He could be a member of an assault company with his rifle only.

"All right, you people, let's go!" the First Sergeant yelled from the top of the ladder. And up they went.

Parry looked different from Engebi. Parry was a longer gray scratch on the horizon and there didn't seem to be so much yellow dust over it, even though the destroyers and cruisers were close in firing their salvos. More palm trees were standing.

Again H. & S. Company was called to the bow net. Without the pestering typewriter Paul climbed nimbly down the ropes and into the rolling LCVP.

But why did they always have to get into the boat so early? Perhaps it had all been planned that way by the Navy psychologists. They got you in the boat early to circle for hours on end so that you would do anything to get out of it. Gladly would you face death just to get off the heaving sea and onto the stable, if bloody, land.

But it seemed to Paul that they did not rendezvous quite so long this time. There they were, bouncing about without direction, when all of a sudden the coxswain shoved the throttle forward and they were on their way to the beach. Landing force make the landing. The red Baker flag had been dropped from the control vessel like a lady's handkerchief in flirtation and now these Marines were on their way to the assault.

The company commander was the only one standing besides the coxswain and his gunner. As he peered at the island his face drained and turned gray. He did not turn to his men and dramatically order them to fix bayonets. Instead he sat down on the deck. The rattle of small-arms fire was very loud, the mortar-bursts close. They seemed to be sailing into this world of noise and explosion whereas at Engebi they had stayed on the perimeter of it. They roared into a bowl of fire. A mortar-burst very close by rained sheets of seawater on them wetting every Marine completely. Their gray-green faces turned to one another.

Like a child the company commander crawled to the stern on his hands and knees. He rose to a kneeling position before the coxswain as if before a shrine.

"Coxswain! What wave we in?"

"Huh?" The coxswain looked down briefly at the obsequious Captain.

"What wave we in?"

"We're supposed to be in the tenth wave."

"What do you mean, supposed to be?"

"Don't give me a hard time, Captain. Things got all fouled up back there at the line of departure. I'm doing the best I can."

This conversation was shouted at the top of their lungs for the LCVP was in the absolute eye of the storm of war. The invisible sounds were so close, so identifiable, that they seemed to be visible solids of noise. The weird and angry flutterings of mortar shells formed zigzag trails above their heads. The explosions about the rocking LCVP were hollow, aching domes of steel. Small-arms fire cracked through the fragile yellow glass of air and the faraway mortar-coughs were the apologetic preludes of a shy man. Again and again seawater fell in solid sheets on them. As protective as young mothers they bent over their weapons, trying to keep them dry.

The machine gunner began firing. What was this? Could he see targets? How could he? Wouldn't he be firing at the backs of the nine waves ahead of them? Neff chewed cigarettes. Leon turned his smooth, pale yellow face and smiled at Paul. They were sitting in water three inches deep.

As they felt the scrunch of sand on the bottom of the boat and the motor roared, the coxswain screamed blood. "Hurry it up! I got to get out of here!"

The ramp stuck. Marines pushed on it. Finally

it gave way and before them, framed by the sides of the LCVP, they saw the exploding beach.

"Get out!" the coxswain screamed frantically, already throwing the motor in reverse, the boat edging back.

And the Marines tumbled down the ramp, holding rifles high, splashing into knee-deep water and up on the beach to hit the sand, to hit that warm, lovely sand and wiggle deeper into it, craning their necks like turtles to look cautiously up and down the beach, then pressing their cheeks against the warm sand, their bodies trembling, wet from the sea.

The beach was crawling with Marines like sea animals making the transition to the land. Hug the sand. Wiggle your hips to dig deeper and deeper into it. What a glorious feeling it was to hug the sand as shells formed speedy steel roofs above their heads. The only home was the sand. Marine after Marine lay on the slanted beach. No one wanted to stick his nose up over the slight ridge just fifteen yards away. Paul knew why LeFort had chosen to remain in the shell hole. Why not?

There was a change in the tone of firing. A harmony was broken. Facing them the island buzzed like a hive of bees upset. But now another buzz was heard. Apart from the rest as if one of the bees had gotten lost. Paul looked up and about him. Other Marines did too, lethargically, as if awakening from a long sleep. Then Paul saw the slugs spurting the sand on their side of the ridge.

"They're behind us," Leon said matter-of-factly, as if he had said, "The sky is blue." He turned. "Nambu in that barge there."

Some twenty-five yards out in the lagoon lay a half-sunken barge. Paul heard the firing. He couldn't associate it with the barge.

"Let's get out of here," Paul said, rising slightly in the pale yellow smoke but hitting the sand again as he heard the sky-whisper of a mortar shell.

"And to where would you suggest?" Leon smiled, nibbling on a candy bar.

But now one Marine, in order to dig into his jacket, casually stood up on the beach. Paul saw that it was Billy, the regimental bartender, who had fought with the assault troops on Engebi. Billy pulled a rifle grenade and launcher out of his jacket, calmly fitted the launcher over the muzzle lugs of his M–1, got down on one knee, jammed the butt of the M–1 in the sand, squinted at the target, in no hurry, squeezed the trigger. There was a crack from his rifle, an explosion on the barge. The firing stopped.

Then the whole blue sky fluttered with mortar shells and earth mushroomed about them. "Mortars on the beach! Mortars on the beach!" came the call, and in tight groups Marines got to their feet and, crouching, ran forward.

"Don't bunch up!" an officer yelled. "Spread out!"

Leon poked him and Paul rose, wondering if he would have if Leon hadn't poked him. They ran up off the beach and over the slight rise and dropped into the first shell hole.

In the shell hole was a dead Japanese. He had already been stripped of emblems, his personal flag. The contents of his pockets were scattered in the sand. Grabbing souvenirs while under heavy enemy fire is a sure sign of veteran troops.

Paul and Leon scarcely took note of the dead man. Their main concern was to get below ground level. But when they were and had a feeling of brief safety, Paul turned to the dead man. The looters had failed to notice a pocket notebook. Paul picked it up. Idly, as if he had all the time in the world, amusing himself on some resort beach in the Caribbean, Paul flipped through the lined pages. All but four were blank. On these were excellent pencil sketches of the ships, their ships in the lagoon, a troop transport, a steaming destroyer, a light cruiser. Paul looked over at the dead man. So he had been lying here in this hole watching their approach, then sketching the ships as they came nearer to shell him and his island. And then this artist had gotten run over by war.

Another Marine dropped into the hole with them. "What are you guys?"

"Huh?" Leon said. "H. & S."

"H. & S.? What are you guys doing ashore now?"

"Don't ask me."

"You're in the first wave, buddy, you know that?"

"We had that feeling."

"Know where Charley Company is?"

"No."

"Gotta find my guys." The Marine rolled over on his back, dug into his breast pocket and hauled out a pack of wet cigarettes. He tossed them to the sand in disgust. Paul handed him his pack that he carried in a Band-Aid tin.

A Marine with a carbine stood above them. "All right, out of that hole, let's go!"

Three pair of disinterested eyes turned on him.

"Come on, move out!"

The Marines in the hole did not stir. The one from Charley Company lighted a cigarette and tossed the tin back to Paul. Paul put the tin in his pocket.

"Don't you hear good?" the carbine Marine said. "Follow me!"

"Know where Charley Company is, Lieutenant?" the Charley Company Marine said.

"It's all fouled up. When we hit the O–1 line you men can find your own outfits."

"I oughta find Charley Company."

"Are you guys going to get out of that hole or am I going to have to blow you out?" The Lieutenant lowered the carbine.

Paul sighed. "Come on, let's go."

Leon said in a small voice, "We're H. & S."

"I gotta find my buddy in Charley Company."

Paul got to his feet. So this was it, at last. Moving up in the assault as a rifleman. But at the rustling of air above them, all the Marines hit the hole again, the officer rolling into the shell hole with the dead enemy and the three Marines. The explosions of mortars turned the air into great hollow pockets of concrete which thrust against their ears and bodies. Shrapnel sang and spat into the sand about them.

"When this barrage is over, we go," the Lieutenant said.

When the mortars were replaced by small-arms fire, the Lieutenant scrambled to his feet. "Let's go!"

The four Marines ran crouched across the torn ground, seeing ahead of them the gray shattered island but no sign of life. A machine gun spoke to them and all four dropped into another shell hole. Breathing heavily, Paul peered over the rim. Something had caught his eye just before he hit the deck. He saw now it was the slight Captain he had first talked to on the airfield on Engebi. The Captain, his helmet in his hand, was calmly leaning against a shattered palm trunk, indicating various enemy positions to his troops. Like a conductor he motioned to a prone Marine. The Marine got to his feet, and holding a light, air-cooled machine gun as he would a rifle, a towel wrapped around the barrel, fired in

short bursts, the gun climbing. Paul thought it would
be confusing not to see target, but the Captain made
it seem less so, made war appear to be almost safe.
He led his men forward until they were merely
ghosts, darting this way and that, in the yellow haze
of explosions.

They were about to move out again when Kelton
ambled up, chewing on a fruit bar. "Thought I saw
that crazy lope of yours, Sergeant," he said to Paul as
he dropped down into the shell hole. "I've got a spot
all picked out for the regimental CP." He turned to
the officer. "These two are my men, Lieutenant."

"I need them."

"So do I."

The Lieutenant glared at Kelton. Kelton's rude
gaze never flickered from the Lieutenant's eyes and
the Lieutenant turned before Kelton did. Kelton
smiled. "These men would be no good to you anyway, Lieutenant." He poked Paul in the ribs with
his foot. "Why this man here is public relations."

The Lieutenant grabbed the Charley Company Marine. "You then, let's go!"

"But my buddy . . ."

"You can join your own outfit when we hit the
O–1 line."

They got up and ran inland. Kelton made himself
comfortable in the hole.

"First time I've been glad to see you, Kelton," Leon said.

Kelton grinned at Paul. "So you finally landed in the first wave."

"Through no fault of ours," Leon said.

"I know."

"I would have . . ." Paul began.

"You would have what, Sergeant?"

Paul looked away.

Kelton nodded inland. "You would have moved up with the Lieutenant, huh?"

"Sure." Paul glared at him.

"And what good do you think you would have done?"

"We could be targets," Leon said.

"Yeah and that's all. Bodies. In the way."

"Why is it the Japs didn't get you on Eniwetok, Kelton?"

"Because the Army was protecting me, that's why. All those nice young draftee dogfaces." He peered up over the rim of the hole. "They're moving up fast." He got to his feet. "Well, come on back. You're out of it now."

The Sergeant Major and the company Captain were bristling about the CP in a large shell hole just up off the beach. Communications men were busy trying to keep in contact with the line companies. The mortar barrage had lifted. Neff was exuberant.

"How about that landing in the first wave, huh? Nothing to it. And no more nights for me."

"What do you mean, no more nights?" Leon asked.

"I get to go to the flagship to sort mail. Waiting for a boat now."

Leon took up his journal pad and went over to monitor one of the TBX's. Kelton checked over his shoulder, then looked about for one of his scouts to send out. Paul felt useless hanging around. He slung his M-1 and walked back down onto the beach. The beachmaster was supervising the unloading of the LCVP's. A first aid station had been set up in a shell hole. The corpsmen were feeding plasma and the doctor moved from man to man, fixing them up as best he could before they would be taken out to the hospital ship.

"Hello there, Marine."

Paul turned at the voice to face a man who he thought at first was an Army officer and a very clean one at that. The officer smiled. "How did it go?"

"Okay," Paul said.

"Land in the first wave?"

Paul nodded.

"Look it." The officer took a notebook out of his pocket. "Could I have your name and hometown address?"

Oh, no, Paul thought. He laughed.

The man frowned. "What's the matter?"

"This is funny."

He looked disturbed. "I'm a correspondent. I'd like to do a story about what you saw, what happened."

"I know, I know," Paul said. "That's what I mean. That's what I am too. A Marine correspondent."

"Oh. Oh. CC, huh?" He smiled and put out his hand. "George Fox."

"From the *Tribune?*" Paul was impressed.

"That's right."

"Pleased to meet you. I've followed your stuff."

"Getting any good stories?"

Paul shrugged. "I don't know."

"This is a hot outfit. I've seen a lot of outfits. You Twenty-second Marines are the hottest of them all."

Paul looked up. "Is that right?"

"They'll get a commendation for this operation."

"You think so?"

"Sure. This battle wasn't supposed to be, you know, not so soon, this Eniwetok. The plan was for Kwajalein, Eniwetok much later. But since the Twenty-second Marines weren't needed on Kwajalein your General devised a quick plan aboard ship. It was inspiring. You're advancing the end of the war by six months."

Suddenly the air tangled with gunfire so close it was like wild barbed wire coiling about their heads.

They dropped to the deck like dead men and through the firing Paul heard Kelton's commands.

"Left! Over to the left! Get down, clowns! Down! Fire left!"

Conducted by Kelton, the carbine and M–1's replied. The small angry battle lasted but seconds.

"Now what was that all about?" said George Fox, rising and dusting himself off.

A group of twelve Japanese, bypassed by the assault teams, dug into covered trenches just a few feet from the command post, had suddenly appeared out of the ground like so many jack-in-the-boxes and taken the CP completely by surprise. Three had rushed forward with bayonets bound to long bamboo poles. The men in the CP were struck dumb. Only Kelton's sharp commands had awakened them to fight and save the lives of the Colonel and his exec.

Now Kelton was squatting in the CP, fitting another clip into his tommy gun. Fox walked up and started talking to him. Bob Voss touched Paul's sleeve. "You got any dope on this guy?"

"Who, Kelton?"

"We're supposed to give the civilian correspondents a hand when we can."

"Oh, sure."

Kelton and Fox were standing very close together now. Paul saw the fury in Kelton's face. Fox looked puzzled. He had put his notebook away.

Voss said, "Didn't see you out at the flagship."

"Couldn't make it."

"Better get on the ball."

"Yeah."

"I filed five stories yesterday."

"Guess I'd better go out there when you do then."

"Sure, man. Good chow. Clean sacks."

Paul saw Kelton grab George Fox by the lapels and snarl into his face. He pushed Fox roughly away from him and turned. With a dazed expression on his white face George Fox came over to Voss and Paul. The three of them walked to the water's edge. Kelton yelled after Paul. "Where you going?"

"I gotta get some stories in."

"Yeah?" Kelton trotted down to Paul. "Listen, Sergeant, you don't put my name in nothing, hear?"

Paul looked at him. "I wasn't planning to."

"Okay." Kelton turned back to the CP. "Have a steak for me."

The three correspondents boarded an LCVP. It was packed with wounded Marines on the wire stretchers with oddly angled limbs, shocked gray faces, spilled yellow sulfa powder on dusty dungarees, some with great bandages over whole faces. Among them the corpsmen moved, making them as comfortable as possible.

They were off the island, out of the war, sputtering out into the blue lagoon. George Fox turned back toward the island.

"What's with that guy anyway? Know him?"

"Kelton? Yes. Why? What happened?"

"He got absolutely incensed when I told him I would like to do a story about him."

Paul frowned. "That's funny. I thought he was the type who would go for publicity."

"Good little story too," Fox said. "He saved a lot of lives, that guy did, a lot of lives with rank."

They were alongside the hospital ship now. The wounded were gently lifted aboard through a great mouth on the side of the ship. Then the coxswain took the three of them, as if they were VIP's, to the sleek flagship where the Marine staff coordinated plans with the Navy Admiral. No nets here. They climbed a gangway, smartly saluting the ensign as they stepped aboard.

Everyone on board appeared to be an officer who had just stepped into the BOQ at Pearl. Clean and noisily starched khakis. Sparkling bars and leafs and birds. The ever-present life belts around their waists added the only wartime touch.

George Fox went to his stateroom to write the overall picture. Bob Voss seemed to know everyone aboard. The clean and shiny naval officers welcomed this grubby little Marine who had been there on the island where the enemy could be seen and touched, the island that they of the Navy had been shelling so impersonally. Voss clapped junior officers on the back as they asked him how the battle was going and he joked with them. "The Marines are winning the war for you swabbies. Our next objective is Dugout Doug." The Navy officers loved it.

They were ushered into the junior officers' lounge and proudly given hot black coffee and seats around a green felt-covered table. It was luxurious. The officers' eyes brimmed with admiration and respect for the two grimy Marines. Paul felt awful. They asked question after question about the landing. Voss could joke about it, but Paul could not. He felt ashamed.

"He needs a typewriter," Voss said to one officer about Paul and this officer snapped to attention.

"Follow me, Sergeant," he said, and they went down a passageway toward the radio shack. Paul felt awkward in his dusty dungarees, the rifle planted on his shoulder, the canteens bumping against his hips as he passed the orderly staterooms and the elegant men in white skivvies stretched out on the clean sacks. How could this be the same war? And if it were, why hadn't LeFort such a job, one where he would never be found out? Certainly LeFort was more of a warrior than these neat and lolling men. And now he was to be punished for desertion under fire. Would these officers hold up any better?

In the radio shack the Lieutenant quickly cleared a desk and uncovered a large, standard typewriter.

"She's all yours, Sarge." He opened a drawer.

"Here's paper and carbon paper." He fussed around Paul the way his mother used to when Paul would return home from college. "Here's an eraser. Pencils and all. I'll see that no one bothers you."

"Thank you, sir," Paul said, unslinging his rifle and propping this crude weapon in one corner of the bulkhead. He took off his helmet and unstrapped his cartridge belt before he sat down. Discreetly the Lieutenant backed out of the door and with a smile said coquettishly, "If you want anything, just whistle."

Paul sat before the typewriter. He rolled in a sheet of copy paper and to test the machine typed, "This is the way the world ends, not with a bang but a whimper." This was a signal machine, all caps with the O slashed. If he thought about listening he could just hear, like conversation in another part of the house, the small-arms firing on Parry. It was all relative, wasn't it? Why was he worrying? How many guys actually pulled the trigger that killed the enemy? How many guys actually saw the enemy to fire at?

The guys in the reserve platoon of an assault company felt guilty because they were not front line. The guys in battalion headquarters felt guilty because they weren't in a reserve platoon of an assault company. The guys in regiment felt bad because they weren't in a battalion headquarters. The guys in brigade felt bad because they weren't in regiment and on board ship the Navy felt guilty because they never went ashore to see the whites of their eyes.

To begin with there is Army and then there is Corps. There are three divisions in a Corps plus a weapons division. There are three regiments in a division and three battalions in a regiment and three companies in a battalion and three platoons in a company and four squads in a platoon and two assault teams in a squad and three men in an assault team. There is one assault team in reserve, two squads in reserve, one platoon in reserve, two companies in the assault and one battalion in reserve and two regiments in the assault and one division in the reserve. Who pulls the trigger?

Paul quickly wrote a piece about Billy, the regimental bartender, knocking out the enemy machine gun on the barge. He wrote about the way Leon built his foxhole and about a Marine bawling because he had stepped on and squashed a lizard.

He had to leave the ship. It was too sterile. Not only that but for some strange reason it was feminine. The slim young officers in their white skivvies. The smell of after-shave lotion. The touch of cool bulkheads, not burst hot sand. The sound of efficiency, not battle confusion.

"Where you going?" Voss asked him in the passageway.

"What do I do with this?" Paul asked him, holding up the sheets of copy.

"Give them to me. I'll file them with my stuff."

"No," Paul said suddenly on impulse, crumpling the sheets of paper in his hand. "They're no good."

"What do you mean, no good? It's copy isn't it. You got names . . ."

"No good. None of it." Paul started to push past Voss.

"What's your hurry?"

"Going ashore."

"Why? Don't be a fool, Paul. We got a deal here."

"Yeah, I know it."

"You're going to get fouled up with PR headquarters."

"I suppose."

Voss shrugged. "Suit yourself."

Paul walked on down the passageway. Out on deck he asked a sailor where the small store was and he went down there. Neff was leaning up against the bulkhead eating ice cream.

"Hi, Paul. Nice boat, huh? Next war I'm joining the Navy."

Paul loaded up on candy bars. In the mess hall he filled both canteens with hot, black coffee and went back topside and flagged the first LCVP back to the beach.

7

Billy

K ELTON WAS SURPRISED to see him. His eyes widened briefly as Paul slipped down into the CP shell hole. Paul passed out candy bars and asked who wanted some good old Navy Joe. Kelton came up and Paul poured him a canteen cup of coffee. Kelton said, "You Red Cross now?" but seemed immediately sorry to have said it. Then he remembered. His eyes flashed.

"That guy write anything about me?"

"No."

"He better not."

"What's with you? What's wrong with a little publicity to feed your ego a little? Not that it isn't fat enough as it is."

"I don't want my name in no damn paper." He turned away.

Parry was just about secured. One enemy strong-hold remained on the southern point. The Colonel wanted the island secured by nightfall and ordered the First Battalion to take the point. But the reply came back from the battalion commander that this would be impossible since because of the narrowness of the point and the fading light he would be firing into his own men. So the Colonel ordered them to dig in for the night, set up defensive positions and expect counterattack. Then the next day at dawn to jump off and take the point. The battalion commander requested more ammunition.

The Sergeant Major stood on the rim of the CP shell hole. "All right, I want volunteers to move ammo."

Paul quickly looked at his feet, as did many others in the CP. He became interested in a smudge on one shoe. Then a terrible kind of casualness came over him and he rose lazily to his feet and slouched against his rifle. "Okay," he said and it seemed to be the last breath in his lungs and he felt weak, but now that he had said it, it was out of his hands and there was no more pondering. A cool breeze blew right through his body. He didn't dare look at anyone for fear his cheek would begin twitching. He wanted to look at Leon but then he heard Leon's voice. "Yeah, okay."

All in all six men volunteered, but only after a few glares by the Sergeant Major. He led them to the ammo dump on the beach. They were each told to

take two metal cases of thirty-caliber machine gun
ammo and a sack of grenades and to report to Captain Duanne at Baker Company which was just down
that way. The Sergeant Major pointed to the south.
"Just keep walking until you run out of island and
that's them."

Trudging along, rifles slung, carrying the ammo
and grenades, in the faded light they crossed the
island. They passed what once were enemy strong-
points and it was as if the assault troops had been
angry gardeners routing the moles from the flower
beds. The island was uprooted. The dead Japanese,
many of them naked and charred black from the
flamethrowers, spilled out of the holes and trenches.

Finally they were on the beach on the sea side.
It was a wide beach and it sloped steeply to the
quiet, coral-filled sea. Beyond this was the edge of
the barrier reef. Here the waves marched in from
deep blue water to be tripped by the reef and explode
in great white plumes. This had been going on for
centuries and to these waves the war was a very small
thing indeed.

"I don't like this time of day," Leon muttered.
He hurried along, stumbling with the weight of the
ammo. "We gotta get back before it gets dark or
we don't get back." He looked at Paul. "How come
you volunteered anyway? If you hadn't I wouldn't
have."

They heard firing ahead of them, then yelling, and saw Marines running down the sand and flopping. Then the thin air ripped about their ears. As one they hit the deck, this party of specialists from H. & S. It had become such an animal instinct that Paul wondered if years later in civilian life when he heard a car backfire he would drop to the sidewalk.

As quickly as it had started it was over. The firing of assault troops was this well disciplined. It began. It ended. There were no confused or eager soloists. The ammo carriers of H. & S. saw the Marines ahead get to their feet. They stayed safely on the ground a moment longer, then rose. Again they trudged up the beach carrying the ammo.

They came across the enemy position. It was an L-trench which had been covered with sheets of corrugated iron, burlap, then sand. In the trench were the seven freshly killed Japanese, too fresh for flies. They were waxen and strangely beautiful with the neat improbable bullet holes in their taut skins. Not mangled. Neatly done. Far better than the broken bodies of a car accident. A classic kill. Their killers were nowhere in sight and had not even bothered with the spoils.

The Japanese slept forever with the small round holes in their taut-skinned faces. Their almond eyes saw no more. A spilled bag of rice. A saki bottle. A personal bursting-sun flag with a flutter of Japanese writing, characters made by a bee which had dipped its hairy feet in India ink and then, numb with morning cold, dragged itself across the silk.

Again Paul thought of the cheapness of their uniforms. Couldn't their quartermaster general have better taste, more money, than to issue them such shabby green cloth? Why couldn't he allow them to die in high style, in splendor and burgundy plumes like knights? There you are you unlucky seven, blind golden mouths open, saki undrunk, flag unfluttered, grenades unblown, cartridges unfired, rice uneaten, bayonets unblooded, lives lived.

The trembling ammo carriers continued on, warily peering up at the top of the remaining coconut palms and into the brush for snipers. But only Marines poked about. Intermittently there would be the warning, "FIRE IN THE HOLD!" and then the tough, dumb thud of a satchel charge.

Close now to the end of the cigar-shaped island they began asking other Marines, "Hey, you guys, where's Baker Company? Hey, you guys, know where Baker Company's at?" The voices were anxious as it grew darker.

"I don't want to spend the night out here," Leon muttered.

Finally they found the CP of Baker Company in a shallow hole. Paul was surprised that line compa-

nies had CP's, then wondered why he should be surprised. The Captain was on the radio. The other
Marines stretched out on the soft slope of the hole.
There was no distinction between officer and enlisted men. Good line officers carried M-1's.

Ahead of the CP the forward troops were dug in
and turned to look at the ammo carriers with hollow
faces. After they put down their burden the ammo
carriers flexed their arms and rubbed their muscles
overtly. Two of the ammo carriers slipped away
so secretly and immediately, no one noticed.

"Good, good," the young Captain said, seeing the
ammo. He turned to his runner. "Flip, see that it
gets to the right people." And the runner jumped
up and carrying two boxes at a time began distribut-
ing the ammo. The forward troops smiled as if they
were being served cake. Paul would have liked to
experience their luxury but it was not in his realm
of thought. The Captain looked at the four remaining ammo carriers.

"We're pretty well shot up here," the Captain
said. He glanced at the sky. "It'll be dark soon. We
need replacements." He seemed to lick his chops.

No one said anything. Paul didn't say anything.

"What outfit you people with?"

Leon said, "H. & S."

"Oh," the Captain said. "H. & S. Well. Well, anyway." He pushed himself to his feet. He was weary

and stooped and terribly old for a young man. "There's something you can do. We got a casualty that's got to go back to the aid station." He climbed out of the shell hole. "Over here."

Dumbly the ammo carriers followed him. The eyes of the assault troops were on the ammo carriers, animal eyes, resentful eyes. Paul believed they hated him more than they did the enemy. Damn you, Paul wanted to yell at the eyes, I could have stayed safely aboard the flagship tonight and had hot chow and slept in a clean sack. But I brought you ammo, didn't I?

And then at Paul's feet was a body, covered with a poncho, helmet off, face turned, skin gray, lying on an improvised stretcher made of another poncho and two long bamboo poles that earlier in the day, with bayonets attached, had been enemy weapons.

"Get him back there before dark or you'll draw fire from your own men," the Captain said. "Know where the aid station is?"

"Yes."

Glad to have this job to do, the ammo carriers now became stretcher bearers, one at each end of a pole. They lifted the casualty, surprised at his weight, and carried him past the foxholes and the quiet, accusing faces. They felt like women, these stretcher bearers did. But now it was all right, or was it? Now it was all right that he hadn't volunteered to stay. Now he had a job to do. Perhaps it was women's work, but if it were, where were the women?

The casualty was heavy. Much heavier than a man should be. Their feet dragged into the soft sand of the exploded and darkening island. But they were going back, back. They left Baker Company and went back.

"That was close," Leon said softly, speaking what was in each of their minds.

"He wouldn't have wanted us anyway, not us H. & S. guys."

"We're bodies, aren't we? We're Marines," Paul said.

"Good old Paul." The casualty turned his head and spoke.

"Huh?" At the head of the stretcher, Paul slowed. This caused the stretcher to bump into his legs, jostling the casualty.

"Take it easy," the casualty said.

Paul looked closely into his face. "Billy!" he cried. "Man, where you hit?"

"Leg."

"Bad?"

"A Stateside hole. A good old Stateside hole."

Paul smiled. "Going home, huh?"

"Yeah, going home."

"Hurt?"

"Naw. I'm in morphine up to my ears. Even feel better now."

"Yeah? How come?"

"You're taking me in, aren't you? My old buddy. Old Paul."

The stretcher bearers continued on. Old Billy. On an operation Billy didn't have to do a thing but sit in the regimental CP and kid the officers about how he used to water their whiskey. But Billy had chosen to fight with the assault troops.

"Let's take a break," one of the stretcher bearers said. "This guy's heavy."

Billy chuckled. "I'm flying, man."

"Keep going," Leon said. "It'll be dark soon."

They stumbled on. He was heavy. It was almost dark. He was too heavy with his Stateside hole. He was going back and they were staying. If it got too dark they would be fired upon by their own men. Damn it, Billy, Paul thought, why didn't you stay with H. & S. where you belonged?

They trudged across the island. Now there was the sound of the first night-fighting. Finally the stretcher bearers reached the CP and passed that to the aid station on the beach.

They pushed through the cool and rustling curtains of the blackout tent and set Billy down. Other casualties were sprawled about under the harsh, cold light of a Coleman lantern. The doctor moved to Billy's side and cut away the bandage on his right leg. There was a small neat hole the diameter of a pencil. It didn't seem real. The doctor cleaned the wound, shook more sulfa powder on it and rebandaged it.

"How is he?" Paul asked.

"Flying," Billy said.

"Clean wound," the doctor said.

"You'll be okay, Billy," Paul said.

The rest of the stretcher bearers had left the aid station. Paul followed and found a shell hole to share with Leon.

Billy died during the night. Paul could not believe it. The morning was bright and warm. The lagoon was blue and Billy was dead. Dead from a hole the size of a pencil in the big part of his thigh. A State-side hole. It couldn't be possible.

The body lay outside the aid station covered with a poncho.

"What happened to him?" Paul asked, grabbing the arm of a corpsman.

The weary corpsman looked at him, at Billy. "Shock," he said.

It could not be. Not from that little hole. And after they had carried him safely all the way back through a combat zone.

"I don't understand," Paul said. "What do you mean, shock? What's that? How could a guy die from such a tiny hole?"

"Doesn't take much."

"But in the leg, the big part of the leg . . ."

"Sorry. He was your buddy, huh?"

"I don't know. Not exactly. A guy I knew."

"Yeah."

"We carried him back last night. He seemed to be okay."

The corpsman stood there trying to think of something to say. Suddenly Paul was angry at Billy for dying. He almost kicked his stretcher. Why the hell did you have to die? Paul turned from the body. He scarcely heard the call to colors. Elements of the First and Third battalions had jumped off at 0600 and had run over the point and wiped out the last of the enemy resistance. Eniwetok Atoll in the Marshall Islands was now completely in United States hands.

8

So Long, Rock

Back aboard the transport Paul was listless and depressed whereas all the other Marines were overjoyed to be once again on steel decks, taking freshwater showers, eating good old Navy chow and above all leaving the atoll behind them to be occupied by the garrison troops.

Paul stayed at the rail as they made the reef passage, escaping from the protective arms of the lagoon. Eight nights ago they had made this same passage and all troops had been ordered below. He stayed watching the islands in the atoll — the ravaged and smoking Parry, but the lovely palms of the unmolested islets.

Then this was all. No more combat until next time. Now what? Garrison duty. Training. More training. Then another beach. The training took so long. Why hadn't he come out of this operation with some kind of attitude he could rely upon? True he had landed in the first wave but that had been a mistake, not his doing, and an officer had had to rout him out of his hole to get him to move up. He had not fired his rifle. He had done nothing to hasten the end of the war. He hadn't even carried Billy back so that he lived.

And his job, what of that? He had not sent one story in. Paul had never felt so ineffectual. So he had chosen when leaving the flagship not to write about it but to go back to the island and do it and fight it, and so what had happened? He had carried ammo, but what was that? Women's work. And he had not volunteered. He had not wished to stay up on the line at night. And he had not been able to carry back an injured man, a friend at that, so that he would be alive in the morning.

Why couldn't there be another island for him to land on tomorrow in the first wave, oh yes, in the first wave, so that he could wipe out this misery forever?

He turned from the rail. A bunch of guys from an assault company were sitting cross-legged on one of the ship's hatches, chattering away as they cleaned their rifles. Paul walked on past them and down below.

The ship steamed south into captured Kwajalein Atoll where the Twenty-second Marines had been held aboard in reserve and were now going for garrison duty.

9

Garrison Duty

Ennubirr was the first perfect atoll islet Paul had been on. There is nothing so fine as a low-lying, palm-swinging islet of a South Pacific atoll. He had seen the miniature beauty of these islets only from the sea. Ennubirr was the dream island, the magazine cartoon of a tropical island, small, not two hundred yards across nor four hundred yards long, thick with glossy green coconut palms and creamy sand and tangled sea grape vines. And perhaps to make it less static, and certainly more romantic, there was one indication of war. A squat, sturdy cement building just off the beach under the palms that the Japanese had used as a power station. There were seven pockmarks on its sides from our five-inch shells. This building was the reason Ennubirr had been given to regimental headquarters. It was here they set up shop, for now their work would truly begin while the conquering heroes, the assault troops, rested and talked battle on the neighboring islands. H. & S.

Company would make out the new muster rolls, send in the KIA and WIA reports, bring the payroll up to date.

They were told to dig in because of expected bombing attacks. A few days before, the Japanese had come over Roi and Namur islands, a few miles to the north, and almost sunk them. Also their good captain, still dressed as if for combat, marched about the island waving his pistol, supervising the foxhole digging and from time to time calling out, "Dig that hole deeper, lad, and expect counterattack from the high seas!"

Paul dug a deep hole on the sea side. Here the breeze was fresh, the ocean blue and rolling in to crash on the barrier reef which lay seventy-five yards beyond the beach. He filled bags with sand and placed them around his home in the ground and he covered the hole with palm fronds. His house looked like a pit to catch animals. Inside it was cool and moist with the sun sprinkling through the fronds.

Leon built a summer cottage. He spent days at it, dragging sheets of corrugated tin and driftwood from all parts of the island. He made tables and chairs from boxes. A pilfered Navy hammock swung in one corner.

Neff was happy now to be sorting his mail and clucking over the ripped and crumpled packages that lay in a great heap in one corner of the mail tent.

Kelton had dug a regulation foxhole on the beach and then disappeared. He was like a beast of prey, foraging somewhere. The hunt was never over for him.

As if out of sight, out of mind, LeFort, with no fanfare of court martial, was broken to Private and transferred to the garrison troops on Roi-Namur. Paul saw him off in the LCVP. LeFort still seemed puzzled. He was not quite sure what he had done wrong. To him it had all been the First Sergeant's fault for transferring him to the assault and not allowing him to stay with H. & S. where he belonged.

Paul explored the island, breathing in the deep and sweet scent of the sea. He found it easy to forget the stench of Engebi and Parry. They were just not the same kind of island. They were merely dusty battlefields plopped in the sea to provide training for the troops. Ennubirr was as lovely as a young girl and he walked her pink beaches and explored her palm groves and swam in the warm water off her lagoon side. No training schedule was set. The officers left them alone and the Marines spent their time building homes in the sand, eating good hot chow served under the palms and washing clothes. Washing clothes was an obsession with Marines. Someone was always washing clothes, in canvas buckets, on homemade stands. Some even built windmills. Paul liked his way the best. He tied a line on his clothes, waded carefully through the shallows to the barrier reef, flung them over and stood there with the line in his hands like a man fishing. He let the breakers pound them for a half-hour or so, then reeled them in. They were clean, certainly salty, and often torn.

The adjutant set up a casual court. He would call in members of H. & S. one at a time to ask them about Roark. When had they last seen him? Had they ever overheard arguments between him and another Marine? Had they noticed anything unusual about Roark's behavior? What did they think? Did he jump? Or was he pushed?

All day long LCVP's ferried in the lagoon between Ennubirr and Roi-Namur where the assault companies were resting, and every other day Paul, like an atoll commuter, took the 0700 boat up to Roi-Namur and the 1700 boat back. On Roi-Namur he talked to the troops and on the days he remained on Ennubirr he typed up his stories.

He got to feeling better about things. He had been able to put Billy in the back of his mind, Billy and all that he involved. Now after the battle was over it seemed all right to do his job.

The troops like to have someone in the know, some officer, or Paul, tell them what they had done. During the battle they were too close to it and knew the sound of a mortar or a slug and the fact that you must get off your gut and move another five yards.

That was all they could think of at a time. Five yards of soil. And to keep down.

The companies were housed in green pyramidal tents on the ruined islands of Roi-Namur, joined by a road on a sand spit, like that hyphen. Paul would go in the tents where the men were lying on cots and talking or writing letters. They got all excited when he asked them questions. It would all come out of them. Paul was a third party. They talked to him the way wives talk to a marriage counselor.

They would call over members of their platoon from other tents. Never did they talk about themselves, just about the battle and what their buddies had done, and their buddies would sit there sheepishly, staring at the deck and grinning.

"This guy here, old Ellison, my buddy, we thought he was crazy. He ran across Engebi like he was out for track and when he was out of grenades he threw rocks."

"Heavy machine gun's no good on a small operation. We never even used tripods on our lights. Just wrapped towels around the barrels and fired them from the hips."

"On Parry," a machine gun corporal said, "we fired twenty boxes of ammo without changing barrels. Fast, you gotta move fast."

"Old baby doll here was the best corpsman I ever did see." The Marine chuckled at the smooth-faced corpsman sitting on the edge of a cot. "Japs must have known he was a corpsman cuz they shot the first aid packet right off his belt."

"Japs," said another Marine, "are such poor shots that if you keep moving you never get hit."

"The nights were the worst. At night the Japs would take off their clothes and put blankets over their heads to break the silhouette."

"On Engebi," a PFC chuckled, "we spotted a Jap calmly riding a bike down the airstrip."

"Yeah, they're all hopped up."

A tall gawky Marine entered the tent. "Hey, Dancer," they said to him. "This guy's going to do a story on you." A Marine turned to Paul. "You know what we call him? We call him the dancing BAR man 'cause he always stood while firing the piece and he would jump and dance about to direct his fire. He looked like one of those jitterbuggers."

"When we first hit Engebi," one of them mused, "I couldn't get it into my head that this was the real thing. I kept thinking that it was just maneuvers."

"To me the loudest noise in the whole operation was when my firing pin clicked on an empty chamber."

"Those Japs are moles. Their trench system on Parry would make the New York subway look sick."

"That blood plasma's okay," a Marine said looking up from the letter he was writing. "Just got a

letter from my girl. She gave some blood. Say . . ."
He smiled. "Wouldn't it be great if I got injured
and got her blood?"

And Paul, his notebooks filled, would leave them
late in the afternoon to catch the boat back to Ennubirr. As soon as he hit Ennubirr he would rush
to his home in the sand and start writing his stories.

Then one evening as Paul sat on an ammo box
outside his hole typing in the cool breeze, the breeze
rattling the copy paper in the roller, Kelton came
up and tossed a sheet of paper in his lap.

"You're fired, buddy," Kelton said.

"Huh?"

"Read it."

Paul read:

HEADQUARTERS
22ND MARINES (REINFORCED)
FIRST PROVISIONAL MARINE BRIGADE, V/AC

15 March 1944

From: The Commanding Officer
To: Sergeant (PR) Paul L. Dean,
            319424, USMC
Subject: Relief from public relations duty
            and reduction in rank
Reference: (a) CMC Serial MC–219312, dated
            1 March 1944

    1. In accordance with reference (a), you are

hereby relieved from Public Relations Personnel and reduced to the rank of Private First Class (Line), Temporary, from and including this date.

Paul's mouth gaped slightly as he read the letter. He felt the sweat in his palms, and then a small stream of it start up under his neck to run down his back. His mouth was dry. He closed it. Finally he looked up into Kelton's face. Kelton stood above him watching him. Kelton wasn't grinning.

"Tough, buddy," Kelton said. "You'll miss that extra forty bucks a month."

"I wasn't thinking of that," Paul said. "That's nothing."

"I know."

"I wonder what happens now."

"Who knows in the lousy Marine Corps?"

"What do I do?"

"Nothing. Just take off your pack and stand at ease. Wait."

"I suppose they'll transfer me to a line company."

Kelton shrugged.

Paul looked at the sheet of copy paper in the roller of his typewriter. The story was about the dancing BAR man winning the war. Well, it wouldn't be his typewriter any more. He'd turn it in. He wouldn't have to worry about lugging it around any more.

"I ought to finish up these stories."

"Why?"

"Well, I took these notes when I was still PR. I ought to write my stories up to date. The guys would be disappointed if I didn't."

"Suit yourself. But I think it's foolish. No one's going to care or know the difference. And it won't get back your stripes."

"I ought to do it."

Kelton picked up his mess gear. "Let's go to chow."

An Offer

PAUL WROTE his stories up to date. He was numb doing them. He handed them in to Lieutenant Jones, the regimental intelligence officer, through whom Paul was sending his stuff.

"I don't understand it," the Lieutenant said as Paul handed him the last of his copy. "You were doing good work. And lots of it. I don't get it."

Paul smiled. "I misspelled February."

The Lieutenant grunted. "But I mean it, Paul."

"I fouled up somehow. I should have sent my stuff through the flagship during the operation."

"You had guard duty. There are other things during an operation besides writing stories."

"My stuff probably isn't any good anyway."

"I think it is." The Lieutenant shook Paul's hand. "Sorry, Paul."

"Thanks."

As Paul was leaving the regimental office the Sergeant Major called him over. The Sergeant Major was a long, lean, red-haired Marine of fifty-five.

"You want a job here?"

"In the office?"

"Sure. I need a man. You can type." The Sergeant Major grinned. "And I like that portable of yours. I could use it. No sense in turning it in to the quartermaster."

"I don't know."

"You want to be thrown out to the line companies? Face it, friend. I know your record. You've done nothing but office-type work since you enlisted."

"I know."

"So you can't tell me you want to go join a line company with a bunch of wild kids and chase around the boondocks and then get shot at in the next operation."

Paul stood there and didn't say anything.

"You got a good job here if you stay with H. & S. I need a man in the paymaster department. Nothing to it. Why in the next operation you might never have to board ship at all but just stay in the rear echelon and keep the payroll up to date."

"I'll think about it."

"Yeah, well okay, but don't take all year."

Now, unassigned, he was nothing. A body in wartime. The word got around that he was broken to

PFC and out of public relations. No one said much. Tough. Leon tried to buck him up and made sense sometimes.

"You're lucky not to have that PR after your name. Wouldn't that look lousy on a grave marker? Sergeant (PR). Now you're line, buddy. PFC (Line)." He clapped Paul on the back. "That'll look a lot better to you when you're dead, won't it?"

And when Leon heard about Paul's chance to join the paymaster department he dropped down into the hole where Paul sat in one dim corner like a prisoner in solitary confinement and said, "Take it. Self-preservation. You're not for the line companies. You're too smart for them. And you'll never make NCO there either. Why I bet in paymasters you'll have your three stripes back in a year."

Paul stayed in his hole or just outside of it most of the time, moving away from the area only for chow. He knew he had better make up his mind soon. He tried to think it out clearly. These were all his friends in H. & S. He had known them for nine months. As paymaster clerk he would be joining H. & S., would not be just an observer as he had been. Someone was going to get the job. Why not he?

Then one morning he noticed Kelton folding up his poncho and cramming it in his pack.

"What's up?"

"Charley Company has been ordered to clean up the bypassed atolls to the south."

"No kidding? I thought we had the Marshalls secured."

"Some of them left. Ebon. Taka. I can't remember all the names. Some of them the Navy's going to bypass. But others have to be secured."

"So you're going along, huh?"

"The Lieutenant gave me permission. Nothing to do here." Kelton strapped down his pack and picked up his tommy gun.

Now Paul felt detached and light-headed. He said it. "I'm going. By God, I'm going too."

Kelton rocked back on his heels and squinted up at him. "At last you're volunteering. But I might have know that if you would do any volunteering at all it would be for a picnic."

"A picnic?"

"Sure. That's all this will be. You know. Friendly relations with the natives."

"You're not sure."

"No. But if there are any Japs they'll probably commit hari-kari."

Paul started to walk back to his hole to get his gear. "I'm going anyway."

"How are you going to go? If you were still PR you could go as a correspondent. But how are you going to go now?"

"As a rifleman."

Kelton chuckled. "You don't know anything about being a rifleman."

"Enough for a picnic."

"You'll be over the hill. You're supposed to stand by here."

"You went over the hill when you joined the Third Bat on Eniwetok, didn't you?"

"That was different." Kelton shouldered into his pack. He looked at Paul. "Well, come on. If you're going, get into your gear."

The Picnic

An hour later they boarded an LST and the miniature task force of one LST, two LCI's and a destroyer glided out of the glassy Kwajalein lagoon and headed south.

There was a carnival feeling among the men. This would be a snap, a cruise, a picnic. An interpreter and a Government man were along to inform the natives that they were now under United States rule. The Marines would be conquerers of a small, warm and friendly world of palm islands.

He heard the voice behind him as he stood at the rail watching the sea. "Well, you going to write us up on this picnic?" He turned to face Captain Jenkins, his pal in college and the hero of Skunk Point on Engebi.

"No," Paul said. "I was kicked out."

"What?"

"Yes."

"How come?"

"Well, there was this Mexican kid in Baker Company named Jesus Mendoza, the Jesus pronounced Hey Zeus, the way they do in Spanish, and I wrote a story about him and my lead was, 'Jesus raised hell with the Japs on Eniwetok.'"

Jenkins grinned.

"Ah hell," Paul said. "I guess I just wasn't good enough."

"Cut it."

"I mean it. I don't know, Pat. It just didn't seem important at the time, when all the firing was going on and guys were getting killed, to get the full name and correct hometown address."

"Yeah."

Paul looked at him. "Can you understand that?"

"Of course I can." He touched Paul's elbow. "You're not in my company now, are you? I mean I haven't seen the duty sheet lately but . . ."

Paul looked down at the rolling blue sea. "No. I just came along."

Jenkins squeezed his arm. "You'll be okay, buddy." He turned and walked down the deck.

They all slept on deck and were awakened before it was light, given powdered eggs and coffee in the tiny mess hall and then marched down the twisting passageways of the ship to the great room at the bow where the amphtracs were. They were to use rubber boats. The big mouth of the ship opened, the ramp was lowered and the troops walked down the ramp and into the black rubber boats.

Paul saw from the action of the sea that they were not in the lagoon but on open sea, some four hundred yards off the barrier reef which in the early light was creamy with the breaking waves. He got into a rubber boat with strangers and felt its cool black skin. They bobbed about in the chop and took up the paddles and headed for the low-lying island, gray in the morning light.

It was better to have something to do such as paddling when you were going to hit a beach, better than sitting stupidly and half sick in an LCVP. He paddled hard and it felt good. The rifle on his back felt good too. There was just that now. No telltale black box. For all they knew he was a transfer, a new man.

The night faded from the sky and the air was fresh with sea. Ahead of them the small islet took on shape and color as the sky blued. They paddled on, the foam and crash of the waves on the barrier reef just ahead of them. The helmsman steered for a section where the shoulders of the waves rounded smoothly and did not explode with such force.

"Hold it," the helmsman said.

They shipped paddles. The water dripped off the paddles onto the smooth surface of the sea. The islet ahead of them appeared to be deserted but for the white birds against the glossy green of the palms. Paul looked over his shoulder. He saw the dark, velvet hump of a wave.

"Paddle!" the helmsman cried. "Hard!"

The rubber boat rose in the swell of the wave, then as they attained the speed of the wave it caught them up in its swollen belly and thrust them toward the reef. The helmsman held the boat steady and did not allow her to broach.

They dropped from the sky, then hit, and bounced once. The wave crashed and foamed about them as they bobbed about in its white water. When it quieted they slipped out of the boat and into water up to their knees. Rifles slung on shoulders, faces blackened, they carried the boat across the shallow water and up onto the beach. There they hid it in a tangle of sea grapes and turned to watch the others land.

One boat capsized. The Marines spilled into the water and the scene seemed to be caught in a camera's flash, bodies and arms and legs, black silhouettes against the pearly sky. There were no casualties.

With muffled thuds of equipment the company grouped under the palms. They all knew what they were supposed to do. Each was a member of a fire team, a squad, a platoon. Even Kelton had a job. He had been appointed by Jenkins to take the point.

Paul felt awkward. He didn't belong anywhere. Kelton nudged him. "Stick with me."

They formed a line of skirmishers with Kelton and Paul in the middle and ahead. They moved across the island as quickly and quietly as possible, peering into palm fronds, bushes and vines snapping and clutching their legs. Paul was a knot of apprehension. There was no talking.

They had landed on the islet south of what air recon claimed was the main island. Now they had covered this small island and had found nothing but its simple and pure beauty. Ahead of him Paul saw the shocking-green sea of the pass and the white beach. Kelton held up one arm as a signal for the troops to halt. Captain Jenkins came up to them.

"We'll go across in twos and threes."

Kelton nodded. Paul turned to look back at the troops. He couldn't see them in the brush.

"How you doing, Paul?" the Captain asked.

"Okay."

"That's the boy."

Kelton and Paul walked down on the sandy beach and into the water. If the enemy were over there hidden in the brush they wouldn't fire until they had more targets. The bottom was white sand spotted here and there with coral heads. Holding their rifles above their heads they waded out into the clear warm water up to their bellies, then stepped into the current and were almost swept off their feet. Kelton grabbed the butt end of his tommy gun and Paul grabbed it. They worked their way across. Now they were on the main island of the small atoll. The palms whispered above their heads. They ducked into the brush and Kelton quickly scouted the immediate area. Finding nothing, he signaled for the rest to come across.

When they had all crossed over and were quietly curled in the brush, Jenkins gave the order to move out again. Halfway down the length of this island Paul and Kelton stopped and crouched. Ahead of them they saw a clearing and warm thatch huts like haystacks. A native man came out of one of the huts and looked at the sea. A small, naked boy dragged a dried palm frond.

Dodging from palm tree to palm tree, Kelton made for the clearing. When he reached the edge of it, he stayed watching for a long time. Then he stood up and casually strolled into the clearing, tommy gun at the sling. When the man saw him he glared. Paul could see the smile on Kelton's face as he walked up to the man and put out his hand. The man did not take it. Kelton offered him a candy bar. The man took that and examined it but did not unwrap it. Kelton peered into one of the huts. Then he walked behind it and around the others. He came back and called to the company, "Send the interpreter."

Paul and another Marine accompanied the interpreter. The natives all came out of their huts and
up off the beach and stood around glaring at the
Marines. "These people are supposed to be friendly,"
the interpreter muttered. The Marshall Islanders
were not as handsome as the Samoans although there
was a Polynesian tenderness in their faces.

While the interpreter talked to the chief, the Marines quickly scouted the area but found no evidence
of the Japanese. The interpreter learned that there
had been a handful of Japanese on the next island
north but that they had left two weeks ago. The
interpreter was puzzled that the people were not
friendly. The Government man ran up the American
flag on a long bamboo pole. The natives were not
impressed. The Marines gave them candy bars and
cigarettes. They accepted these, holding them in their
hands. Finally the interpreter learned that the day
before, a box had washed ashore. In it had been a
hand grenade. A child had found the box and played
with the grenade. It had exploded, killing the child.
The natives held the Marines responsible.

The interpreter tried to explain to the people that
it was not the fault of the Marines. They would not
believe him.

"It's too bad," Captain Jenkins said, "that we
can't stick around and try to make them understand.
But we don't have time. We got to secure this atoll
before dark."

The Marines moved on down the length of the main island to the pass and crossed it as before. On the next islet they saw where the Japanese had been, the matted fronds under the palms, and the remains of their cooking fire. They continued on and completed the circle of islets. Captain Jenkins called the atoll secured. They boarded their rubber boats and paddled out to the waiting LST.

On the next atoll the natives made it almost impossible for the Marines to move. They clung to them with happiness and love. They prepared a feast of pigs and chicken and fish. They sang their songs for them and danced on the sands of the beach.

But there was work to do. Forming a line of skirmishers, they circled the islets and, finding no evidence of the enemy, called another atoll secured and paddled back out to the LST.

On the next atoll the chief told the interpreter that there were Japanese on the second island down.

Paul was excited. Now at last he could wipe everything clean. Or could he? At least he would know what he was. He was in the point with Kelton. They crossed the main island and waded the pass. Not this islet. The next one. Paul could feel the tenseness in the troops. They were quiet, their canteens thumping softly against their hips. There was the pass ahead of them. That islet was it. Kelton and Paul waded the pass. They ran up the beach and dived into the brush. "Down, down," Kelton whispered to Paul. "Move ahead using butt plate and knees."

Paul crawled through the brush five yards to the right of Kelton. It was hot. Twigs snapped against his face. His knees were raw and he felt as if someone were sitting on his back. He peered ahead through the brush and suddenly he didn't want to do this any more. Without even realizing it, he stopped crawling. It was pleasant here. He would lie here for a while and then perhaps later on find a coconut to drink.

"Come on!" Kelton's voice snarled back to him.

Wearily Paul drew up one knee, pushed ahead with that, drew up the other.

"Look alive!"

"All you want to do is kill, kill, kill."

"What?"

"Nothing."

They crawled on. Paul hoped it would be over soon whatever it was. They crawled on for some forty yards more and then Kelton stood up behind a palm tree and looked all around. As Paul lay on his belly in the brush breathing heavily he became sleepy.

"I'll get the rest of them," Kelton said, and turned, and was gone. Now Paul was alone out there. He stayed timidly on the ground like a quail. He remembered how they could appear from out of the

ground like magic. Could he possibly fire his rifle?
He was alone and it was too quiet and he was sweating so much it seemed he would sweat all of himself outside himself so that when Kelton returned
all that would be left of him would be a uniform, a
rifle and a pool of sweat drying in the sun. It was
difficult to focus his eyes through the brush. He
kept focusing them on things close by, twigs and
copra bugs hopping about. They were lucky, copra
bugs were. He had to blink and widen his eyes to
look past this to where he didn't want to look.

But then he heard movement behind him and
Kelton's whisper, "Move out." Somehow he got
moving again. Then Kelton stood up. And somehow
he stood up too.

They moved ahead, keeping down, using cover
and concealment, bayonets fixed, safeties off. Paul
felt dreamy. Kelton's arm shot up and they all
dropped to the deck. What had he seen? Kelton crept
forward. Then he slowly got to his feet, sighed and
motioned that it was okay.

The enemy were sprawled about their campsite
and they were all very very dead. They had taken
off their shoes and had tied strings to their big toes
and to the triggers of their rifles and they had held
the rifle muzzles under their chins and blown the
tops of their heads off. They were very very dead.
Nine of them.

12

A Small War

PAUL FELT CHEATED. He had worked himself up
to facing the enemy and then there was no enemy.
He felt that he could have faced them then. He had
forgotten, as all men will, his thoughts when alone
in the brush. Now he doubted if he could work himself up to that high a pitch again, the way he was
when he was moving forward as a member of, a
member of what? Of Kelton. It wasn't humanly possible.

He stood at the rail of the LST as it steamed
toward the last atoll in the darkness and looked over
the stern at the screws churning up the blue-white
balls of phosphorescence. Most of the troops were
down below playing cards. They were joyous. This
was a picnic. And this last atoll. There wasn't even
a native settlement on it so how could there be
enemy. And after this they would go back under
battalion control at Kwajalein, then maybe after
that to Pearl and liberty.

How long would it be then before Paul would find out just exactly what he was?

"I guess you did the wrong thing, buddy," Kelton said at his side.

Paul turned to look at him.

"Should have stayed on Ennubirr and taken that job in the paymasters. You're going to get all fouled up now."

"I don't care."

"You should care. You know how it is in the Marines. Don't fight the stream. You get in bad trouble when you do. Move by instinct and with it. This decision of yours to come along on this trip was the wrong one and it didn't prove anything anyway, did it?"

The following morning at dawn they were faced with a similar string of islets and again they landed on the barrier reef side in their rubber boats. Kelton and the Captain tried to keep the chatter and laughter of the troops down as they moved across the first island.

Carelessly they moved across the second island in a line of skirmishers. Kelton and Paul were at the point. Kelton was far from careless. He moved quietly and quickly, always suspicious.

The burst of firing caught Paul unaware and he just stood there, gazing stupidly about him.

"Down!" Kelton spat at him from where he lay and Paul dropped to hear the slugs snap into the

bushes and thunk into the palm trunks. Kelton
opened fire. What did he see? Or weren't you supposed to see anything?

Tud tud tud, went Kelton's tommy gun, the
empty cartridges clanging out of the chamber, the
sun glinting on their golden cases.

Kelton turned to him. "Keep me covered." And
he got to his feet to run back to the troops as now
Paul unsnapped the safety of his rifle and for the
first time in this operation, for the first time in this
war, opened fire, the rifle bumping him solidly in
the shoulder, the empty cases clanging out. He fired
a whole clip before he knew it, aiming into the
brush ahead of him, then dug in his bandolier and
jammed in another clip.

Behind him and on either side he heard them
bringing up the light machine guns. Kelton crawled
back to Paul's side. Now the air was sweet with the
smell of the firing. He heard the slight cough, the
rustle and the explosion behind.

"Knee mortar," Kelton said.

Kelton crawled ahead. Then to be close to Kelton
more than anything else, Paul crawled ahead too,
toward the stuttering of a Nambu. Another cough,
another explosion. After it Paul turned to see Jenkins
behind him directing his men into positions. Then
Jenkins dashed forward and dived to the ground by
Paul's side.

"How many?"

"I don't know."

Kelton turned back. " 'Bout thirty to forty of them best I can figure out. In fire trenches."

"They got us zeroed in with their mortars."

"We'll take 'em."

"Where are the MG's?"

"On either flank."

"Good. I'll keep them firing."

"Give me a couple squads, Captain. Paul and me'll move in with grenades. I could use a BAR man."

"Okay."

Kelton was shaking Paul's shoulder. "Come on."

It was very noisy. Everyone in the world was firing over his head.

"Huh?" Paul said.

"Come on."

"Yeah."

"You got grenades?"

"No."

"Oh, for God's sake. Here." Kelton unstrapped two from his pack and handed them to Paul. Paul looked at the grenades in his hands.

"Let's go," Kelton said.

Kelton and Paul crawled ahead. It was awkward carrying the grenades and the rifle. On their flanks their machine guns spoke. Another cough, another rustle. Then someone was on top of Paul smothering him and he thought, Is this a Jap? but there was no time to think further as the explosion rose in front of him and dirt fell all about him.

Kelton rolled off Paul's back. "Close," he said.

"You get hit?" Paul asked, seeing the bloody hand of Kelton.

"Naw."

They moved ahead.

"Okay," Kelton said. "Hold it." He unclipped a grenade from the strap of his pack. Paul peered through the brush. He saw a helmet, yes, he saw a tinny green helmet. Right there. They were close. He saw the flash of sun on glasses. They were twenty yards away. They stuck the muzzles of their rifles over the trench and fired. What the hell. Paul jerked his rifle to his shoulder and fired a clip. Then calming down a bit he inserted another clip and began to take aim.

"Grenade!" Kelton spat. In a long lobbing motion Kelton tossed his grenade. Paul pulled the pin of his and, as if he had done it a hundred times, tossed it. Two orange flashes bloomed up before them.

Kelton had another grenade ready. "After this one, we go," he said.

"Huh?" Paul said.

"What's the matter, don't you hear good?"

Kelton and Paul tossed their grenades and after the explosion Paul heard "GO!" and he looked up and Kelton was on his feet and then magically Paul found himself on his feet too, yelling his throat sore, firing from the hip, charging through the smoke and the firing, yelling insanely, firing into their faces. He yelled with a fury he had never known before as he fired alongside Kelton at the faces blooming before him and then something spun him around and knocked him flat.

The Rifle

PAUL CAME TO on the beach. His head throbbed. The sun was hard and hot in his face. He sat up and felt dizzy and lay down again with his arm over his face.

The corpsman came over. "How you feel?"

"What happened?"

"Got a crease in the skull. Not bad."

Paul put his hand up and felt the bandage there. "How's Kelton?"

"Who?"

"The platoon sergeant."

"Oh."

"Oh what?"

"He's . . ."

Paul sat up and looked about. "Where is he?"

"Take it easy now."

"Is that him there?"

"Yes."

Paul crawled over to Kelton. He had been hit in the gut. They were pouring plasma into him. Kelton looked up when he felt Paul was near. "Man, that morphine. I'm flying. How you doing?"

"Okay."

"You're a wild man."

"Yeah?"

"Yeah . . . Say, Paul . . ."

"Yes?"

"I got a feeling they're just making me feel good."

"Naw."

"I mean it. Listen. Come close."

Paul leaned over Kelton.

"I tossed Roark over the side. Why the hell not?"

"Yeah, why the hell not?"

"He was no good to anybody but I still don't know why I did it. We got arguing about who won the World Series in 1933 and I got mad and I just tossed him over the side. Why not?"

"You're right. Why not?"

"Sure." Kelton turned his head away with the pain.

The corpsman said, "Hey no talking, Sarge, huh?"

Kelton grinned at the corpsman. "Okay, baby, anything you say." He turned to Paul again. "Another thing as long as I'm on it. The reason I didn't want my name in no damn paper is that I got into a little trouble in Australia and I just, well, didn't want my name in the papers."

"Everyone's got to get into a little trouble once in a while."

"Yeah, well, this was a little trouble all right." He blinked at Paul. "I don't know, after Guadalcanal it didn't seem to make any difference."

"Okay, here you go." Another corpsman came up and they got on either side of the stretcher.

"See you, Paul old buddy," Kelton said, as they started to carry him away down the beach to the waiting LCVP.

"Sure."

Paul caught the corpsman's eye. The corpsman slowly shook his head. They carried Kelton aboard and that was the last Paul ever saw of him.

Back out at the LST the doctor redressed Paul's crease. He told him to go to his sack and lie down. But Paul went topside and breathed in the air and looked at the islet where the small war was held. It didn't look like a place where people had been killed. It looked very lovely. Then the LST got underway and this view was taken from him.

He was surprised to find the rifle still in his hand, the muzzle lightly in his right palm, the butt plate on the deck as if it had grown from his hand. He lifted it off the deck and looked at it and remembered its number, 88625. It was dirty. He opened the bolt and looked down the barrel. Man, it was dirty. He turned to the bunch of Marines sitting cross-legged on the hatch cover, joking and laughing and cleaning their rifles with hot water and soap.

"Hey, buddy," one of them said to him. "You got any extra rifle patches?"

"Sure," Paul said, joining the group.

THE SECRETARY OF THE NAVY
Washington, D. C.

The Secretary of the Navy takes pleasure in commending the

TWENTY-SECOND MARINES, REINFORCED, TACTICAL
GROUP ONE, FIFTH AMPHIBIOUS CORPS

consisting of:

Twenty-second Marines, Second Separate Pack Howitzer Battalion; Second Separate Tank Company; Second Separate Engineer Company; Second Separate Medical Company; Second Separate Motor Transport Company; Fifth Amphibious Corps Reconnaissance Company; Company D, Fourth Tank Battalion, Fourth Marine Division; 104th Field Artillery Battalion, U.S. Army; Company C, 766th Tank Battalion, U.S. Army; Company A, 708th Amphibian Tank Battalion, U.S. Army; Company D, 708th Provisional Amphibian Tractor Battalion, U.S. Army; and the Provisional DUKW Battery, Seventh Infantry Division, U.S. Army

for service as follows:

"For outstanding heroism in action against enemy Japanese forces during the assault and capture of

Eniwetok Atoll, Marshall Islands, from February 17 to 22, 1944. As a unit of a Task Force, assembled only two days prior to departure for Eniwetok Atoll, the Twenty-second Marines, Reinforced, landed in whole or in part on Engebi, Eniwetok and Parry Islands in rapid succession and launched aggressive attacks in the face of heavy machine-gun and mortar fire from well camouflaged enemy dugouts and foxholes. With simultaneous landings and reconnaissance missions on numerous other small islands, they overcame all resistance within six days, destroying a known 2,665 of the Japanese and capturing 66 prisoners. By their courage and determination, despite the difficulties and hardships involved in repeated reembarkations and landings from day to day, these gallant officers and men made available to our forces in the Pacific Area an advanced base with large anchorage facilities and an established airfield, thereby contributing materially to the successful conduct of the war. Their sustained endurance, fortitude and fighting spirit throughout this operation reflect the highest credit on the Twenty-second Marines, Reinforced, and on the United States Naval Service."

All personnel attached to and serving with any of the above units during the period February 17 to 22, 1944, are authorized to wear the NAVY UNIT COMMENDATION RIBBON.

JOHN L. SULLIVAN
Secretary of the Navy

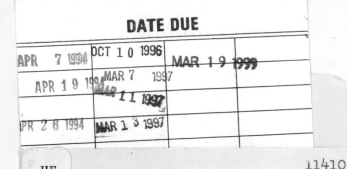